FRIGHTMARES 2

MORE SCARY STORIES FOR THE FEARLESS READER

Frightmares 2 is published by Stone Arch Books
A Capstone Imprint
1710 Roe Crest Drive
North Mankato, Minnesota 56003
www.mycapstone.com

© 2016 Stone Arch Books

Library of Congress Cataloging-in-Publication Data is available
on the Library of Congress website.

Summary: What if a monster lived inside your mailbox? What if your school
had a cursed locker that made its owners go missing? What if you rode on
a haunted roller coaster? In each of the tales in this book, people are afraid.
Very afraid. Read their stories. See if you share their fears. Because if you
don't now . . . you will.

ISBN: 978-1-4965-4136-9 (paperback)
ISBN: 978-1-4965-4421-6 (reflowable epub)

Designer: Hilary Wacholz
Image Credits: Dmitry Natashin

Printed in Canada.
009647F16

FRIGHTMARES 2

MORE SCARY STORIES
FOR THE FEARLESS READER

BY MICHAEL DAHL

ILLUSTRATED BY XAVIER BONET

STONE ARCH BOOKS
a capstone imprint

TABLE OF CONTENTS

Dear Reader,

When I was young, there was an old, shadowy tree right outside my bedroom window. At night the shadows made weird, unsettling shapes, and I was convinced two blackbirds with sharp beaks were sitting on the branches, staring at me.

My mother had to pull down the window shade every night to help stop my nightmares.

I also thought there were bears living in my closet. And each night they tried to come out.

At the time, we lived across the alley from a funeral home. One afternoon, a man who worked there asked my father to help him unload a delivery from a truck. New coffins.

I guess I've always been around strange stuff. It's part of my blood, my brain, and my dreams.

And a few **NIGHTMARES** . . .

Michael Dahl

SECTION 1

DON'T LOOK BEHIND YOU

THE
FLOATING
FACE

Iris tightly gripped the books to her chest.
Her long black hair swirled about her face.
Her school uniform skirt flapped against her
knees. She didn't remember the wind being
this strong when she walked to the library
right after school. But when the library closed
for the night and Iris, the last one out, stepped
onto the sidewalk, a gust of wind greeted
her, a gust full of soot and grit that roared
in her ears and made her shut her eyes. The
rough breeze swept through the streets,
ripping newspapers out of people's hands and
knocking over garbage cans.

Iris hadn't been watching the clock or paying attention to her phone. She had been busy skimming through books for her history report that was due tomorrow morning. And now she was late for dinner.

Iris got a better grip on her books and then set off down the sidewalk for home.

A block from the library, she waited for the light to cross the street. A pale piece of paper rolled and twirled down the street toward her. It never touched the street but danced and floated a foot above the ground. Iris was still waiting for the light as the paper blew nearer.

There was no one else around. Not even any cars. Iris decided to walk across, and that's then she noticed the paper. It floated above the street and drifted toward her legs.

Iris expected it to be a square piece of paper, but instead it was round. Then Iris gasped. It was a paper face. A pale forehead, two curving eyebrows, slits for eyes, a sharp nose, parted lips, and a little white chin. *It must be a mask,* thought Iris. The paper face danced around her, caught in a whirlpool of air.

Iris walked across the street and the face followed. It never fell to the ground. It never touched her. Instead, it bobbled and glided around the girl. When Iris reached the other side and continued down the sidewalk, the face never left her side.

At one point she reached out to grab it, but the wind pushed it beyond her reach. Then she stood still and watched it circle around her.

Once more Iris reached out, but then she quickly drew her hand back. The floating face smiled at her. The thin pale mouth actually moved. And as she continued to watch, the mouth moved faster and faster in the moaning breeze. No longer smiling, it frowned, then grimaced. It opened wide, revealing a set of teeth.

Iris screamed and ran.

The paper-thin face floated behind her, never more than a few yards away.

"Somebody help!" called Iris. "Somebody!"

But she was alone. The streets were dark and empty. Only the wind and the wavering face kept her company.

Finally, Iris saw a teenaged girl up ahead, waiting at a bus stop.

"Help!" called Iris. "Please help me." The girl was turned away from Iris, watching for the bus. But when she heard the cries for help she turned. Then Iris screamed louder.

The other girl had no face. Where her eyes and nose and mouth should have been was a pale white surface, smooth as an egg.

Iris watched as the face glided toward the girl, who bent down and reached out. The papery face, like a tame bird, gently came to rest in the girl's hand. Iris watched in complete disbelief.

The face, still in the girl's hands, moved its lips. "Thank you for finding it," it said to Iris. "I lost it in the wind."

The girl pushed the face onto her head, but now it was more horrible. The face had attached itself to the girl upside-down. Her eyes were blinking on her chin, her mouth was near her hair. The girl laughed.

"Oh dear," she said. "I'll just have to adjust it —" Then she stopped. The upside-down eyes fixed Iris with a cold stare.

"No," said the girl. "I don't think so. I think, instead, I'd rather have *your* face. It's so pretty."

WHAT THEY FOUND IN THE ALLEY

Cars from the nearby streets have gone silent. There are no chirping birds. No rumbling planes overhead. No humming of machinery or workers' voices from inside the warehouse. It feels wrong to him. He realizes he can't even hear his feet scraping against the ground.

Chip can't even hear himself breathing. He feels like he's inside a giant aquarium.

As he trots along, the silence and the darkness grow deeper and deeper.

When he reaches the end of the alley, Chip feels different. But he doesn't have time to think about it. He hears the bell ringing outside the school, and he knows that he needs to get to class!

He runs to his science class and plops down in his assigned seat. He made it just in time!

During class, Chip is quiet and listens to the teacher, which is something he does not do every day.

After class, the teacher, Mr. Salah, asks Chip to stay behind for a minute. Chip stands obediently as Mr. Salah returns to his desk.

"Chip," says Mr. Salah, "are you feeling okay this morning?"

"Yes," says Chip.

"Is everything all right at home?" asks Mr. Salah gently.

"Yes," says Chip.

Mr. Salah smiles. "It seems as if something may be bothering you, Chip. You're normally not this quiet in class, you know." Mr. Salah tries to make it sound like a joke.

"Sorry," says Chip.

"Nothing to be sorry for, Chip," says Mr. Salah. "Some days we don't feel like ourselves. It happens to everyone. Sometimes we get up on the wrong side of the bed. Or we change our routine."

Chip looks up at the teacher. Mr. Salah is a bit startled. The boy's eyes look dark and empty.

"The alley," says Chip.

Mr. Salah is confused. "Alley?"

"I took a short cut through the alley."

"I see," says the teacher. "Do you always go through the alley?"

Chip shakes his head slowly. Then he says, "I found something there."

Mr. Salah leans forward. "Oh? What did you find?"

The boy lowers his eyes and remains silent. The teacher sits back in his chair and waits. Chip won't talk.

"All right, Chip," he says. "You can go. But let me know if there's anything you need help with."

"Okay," says Chip. He picks up the books on his desk, opens the door, and then walks out.

As the door closes behind Chip, Mr. Salah shakes his head. He is puzzled by the boy's odd behavior. He walks over to the classroom windows and gazes across the school parking lot toward the huge, sprawling warehouses. If he stares hard enough, Mr. Salah can just make out the entrance to the alley.

He's heard strange stories about that alley, but there's no way they could be true. The biggest rumor is that the alley has a portal to an alien realm, but not everyone is picked to enter the portal.

Once the last school bus has left, Mr. Salah grabs his own backpack and walks toward the alley.

The look in Chip's eyes has been bothering him all day. Mr. Salah is also bothered by what the boy said. What did he find in the alley?

The teacher hesitates at the entrance to the alley. It is quiet, and the shadows creep up the walls as the sun slides lower in the sky. Mr. Salah checks his watch. He is going to time how long it takes to walk through the alley. He takes his first step. It is only a matter of minutes until he is deep inside the alley. The sound of his footsteps grows quieter the farther he goes.

It is getting dark. There is no one near the entrance to the alley. No one to see the burst of red light. No one to hear a voice cry out suddenly and then stop.

Chip is nowhere near the alley. He doesn't see the burst of light or hear the cry. But he doesn't have to. He knows what happens to Mr. Salah. He knows what the man found.

Or rather, he knows what found him. The same thing that Chip found.

Chip is in his bedroom now. It is late and time for bed. Once he closes the door, he goes to sit down on the bed. He puts his hands on his ears, then he carefully unscrews his head from his neck. The boy gently places the head beside him on the covers. He reaches inside his neck and pulls out a long, thin antenna.

The antenna begins to hum. A voice crackles through the air in Chip's bedroom.

"Replacement robot of young humanoid reporting. All clear. Repeat, all clear. The invasion may now proceed to Phase Two."

THE GOBLIN
IN THE
GRASS

Lisa stood at her bedroom window, watching moonlight turn the backyard into a sea of silver. A movement in the center of the lawn caught her attention. A creature covered in shaggy fur was crawling out of the ground.

Lisa didn't scream or yell for help. She didn't move. She stood there, watching. The creature's head turned quickly. It had caught her spying on it. The thing ran toward the house, and as it ran it grew tall enough for its face to be level with Lisa's.

It stared at her through the window. Its eyes poked out of its head on long, fleshy stems. Lisa saw, close up, that the creature's shaggy hide was actually grass. Suddenly, the creature opened its jaws. The mouth was a huge, hollow blossom, with three separate tongues unfurling from its bloody red throat.

Lisa woke up with a shout. It was morning, and sunlight was pouring into her bedroom. Her window was open, and she heard the sound of the lawnmower. She smelled the fresh aroma of cut grass. She quickly dressed and hurried outside.

Lisa lay on a lawn chair on the patio. She hoped the sunshine and fresh air would help drive away the fear that lingered from the dream. She'd had nightmares before, but this one troubled her more than she wanted to admit.

As she lay there, soaking up the warm sunlight, she remembered a story her grandmother had told her. A story about a powerful creature that lived underground.

"The goblin in the grass," her grandmother called it.

The creature, made of grass and bark and flowers, lived within the earth. It shunned the humans, but it could grow dangerous and come above ground if it felt its home was threatened.

Lisa's father had finished mowing the lawn. Now he was in the yard spraying weed killer. *Poison,* Lisa thought. *That's what weed killer is. So what happens to the poison once the weeds are dead? Does it seep into the ground, deeper and deeper? Does it stay there forever, like a dark, oily underground lake?*

Lisa shook her head. She had dreamed about the grass goblin because somehow her grandmother's story had stuck in her brain. And because she'd smelled the grass through her open window.

Maybe some plants do get poisoned, she told herself. Maybe they grew twisted and ugly, or even deadly to the touch. But that didn't mean they would turn into a creature that could crawl up out of the grass.

Lisa walked into the house to have breakfast. Her mother was not in the kitchen as usual, which was strage.

"Mom!" called Lisa.

Probably at the neighbors, thought Lisa. Her mother was proud of their garden. In the summer she loved to bring her gorgeous blooms to friends and neighbors. Lisa grabbed some orange juice, then walked into the front hallway.

On a table next to the front door sat a huge vase overflowing with her mother's flowers. Lisa had to admit they were beautiful. Purple, green, and orange blossoms mingled with golden leaves and bright red ferns. Lisa didn't recognize any of the flowers, which was odd because she sometimes helped her mom in the garden.

Lisa felt a little light-headed. She could swear the flowers were moving. Several orange blossoms rose up from the middle of the vase. They rose higher and higher and slowly drooped forward, and then hung there like two neon eyeballs staring her in the face. The blood-red leaves were shifting back and forth. They fluttered in a sudden breeze. Lisa froze as she saw two hairy green arms burst out from the leaves and reach for her throat. Then she blacked out.

"Lisa . . . Lisa, honey . . ."

The girl slowly, painfully opened her eyes. It was too bright. Her mother and father were staring down at her. But where was she? This wasn't the front hallway.

"How are you feeling, honey?" her mother asked.

"Where am I?" Lisa mumbled.

"Don't worry. You're at the hospital," her dad said. "You're doing okay. You just fainted."

Lisa didn't understand. She shook her head.

"I found you in the hall," her dad said. "The doctor thinks there's a gas leak in the house. We're having someone look at it."

"You'll be fine," her mother said. "You already look so much better than you did when — when we got here."

"A gas leak?" Lisa said.

Her mother nodded.

"It can be dangerous," said her dad. "That stuff is like poison. It can knock you out, or make you see things."

See things? thought Lisa. *Like plants moving, or green arms reaching out of flowerpots?*

Lisa took a deep breath. She did feel better. Afternoon sunlight gleamed on the metal frame of her hospital bed and the snow-white sheets.

"Can I go home?" she asked.

Her mother smiled. "Tomorrow," she said. "The doctors want you to stay overnight, so they can make sure it's all out of your system."

Her dad patted her arm. "We've been here for a while, kid. I hope you don't mind if we run down to the cafeteria and get something to eat. We'll be right back. Do you want anything?"

Lisa shook her head. She waved as they stepped out of the room.

The girl leaned back against the soft white pillow. She sighed. *What a weird day,* she thought. First the nightmare, then she'd fainted from a gas leak. She had been so silly earlier. Flowers don't attack people.

Her mom popped her head into the room. "By the way," she said. "I hope you like the flowers I brought from the garden. I thought they'd cheer you up. Be back soon."

Lisa turned and looked toward the other side of the room. A huge pot of brilliant blossoms stood next to the window. The window was closed, but Lisa saw the flowers sway in a breeze. They shifted back and forth. Back and forth.

THE
WRONG
BUS

Lora stood at the bus stop and yawned. Another dull, gray morning. The rain clouds looked like they would burst any minute and soak her to the bone. Had her dad told her to take an umbrella? She couldn't remember.

It was only Wednesday, and Lora was dead tired.

She barely remembered getting out of bed, putting on her clothes, eating a toaster snack, grabbing her backpack, and heading out the door. She did it every day, without thinking. Somehow, with her eyes half open and her shoes untied, Lora lumbered across the busy street and waited for the bus.

Lora stood at the bus stop and listened to the morning sounds. People walking past. Kids talking to each other. Dogs barking. Car horns. A siren rushing off into the distance.

Lora looked up and down the street for the siren but didn't see it. Suddenly, the bus was right in front of her, its door open, waiting for her to climb on. She had been looking for the siren so intently that she missed hearing the bus squeak to a stop, like it did every morning. Lora sighed. She hiked her backpack onto her shoulder and trudged up the bus steps. She was looking down at her loose laces and the dirty floor when the bus driver startled her.

"Grab a seat, kid."

It was a new driver. His face was so full of wrinkles, she couldn't tell if he was smiling or not. *Hope the old guy can see the road,* Lora thought as the door shut with a loud screech. There was a rattle and a cough, and the bus pulled away from the curb.

Lora found the last empty seat. Not her regular one, but one near the back. The other girl sitting there did not slide over. She wanted to be on the aisle. She barely moved her knees so Lora could squeeze in and sit by the dirty window. Lora didn't recognize her.

Lora yawned again, then looked around.

She didn't recognize any of the other students. Maybe she had missed her regular bus.

Lora turned toward the window, but the glass was coated with frost. Lora hadn't realized how cold it was. She cupped her hands together and blew on them. *The heater must be broken,* she thought. Lora put her fist on the glass and wiped at the frost. After a few moments, she could see green rolling hills and plenty of trees without leaves. Where were they? And how had they gotten out of the city so quickly?

She heard the girl next to her. "Don't worry. This is the right bus. We'll get there in time."

Lora turned. The girl's face was pale. Her lips were blue as if she had been standing out in a blizzard. Her eyes were empty sockets. Her mouth barely opened when she spoke. "We'll get there. The cemetery is only a few more miles."

"Cemetery?" croaked Lora. "I thought this was the school bus."

"It is," said the girl.

The bus lurched to a stop.

"Everybody out," cried the bus driver.

All the students stood up and shuffled down the aisle to the door. Lora was last. When she climbed off the bus, her shoes touched a dirt road instead of the school's black asphalt parking lot. Behind them stood a tall gate of black metal, with stone walls stretching on either side. In front was a wide green lawn dotted with fallen wet leaves. Among the leaves were several dozen tombstones, new and white. Lora watched as all the students walked.

The girl with the blue lips who had sat next to her walked up to a tombstone. When the girl reached it, she turned and looked back at Lora.

"You don't want to be late for school," she said. Then the girl slid down into the ground, as if she were standing on a trapdoor.

Lora watched as all of the students, each at a separate grave, were sucked into the grassy ground, one by one, until she was alone.

She turned. The bus was gone. The metal gates were closed behind her. Then she heard a familiar sound. A school bell was ringing somewhere. Somewhere deep underground.

THE NOT-
SO-EMPTY
TENT

The Tropical Ranger Scouts from Tallahassee, Florida, were cleaning up a section of highway on a hot, sticky July morning. They had only been working an hour but already everyone was sick and tired of Avery Cooper.

"Don't step on that!" Avery shouted a fellow scout, Henry. "That's a *Carnadina muscaria*!"

"Huh?" said Henry.

"A red-tooth mushroom," explained Avery. "They're very rare. Step around it when you pick up trash!"

Avery waved his hands at another scout. "Don't put your bag down there," he said.

"Those furball ferns are delicate. They've only been blooming for a week."

"Got any ideas where I *should* put it?" asked Ben, another scout.

Avery, hands on his hips, looked up and down the highway ditch they were working in. "Terrible. This is just terrible," he said. "We are destroying this ecosystem."

"Which is why we're cleaning up the garbage," said Henry, tossing an empty pop can into his plastic bag.

"No, no, we shouldn't even be here," said Avery. "We're damaging the grasses and the plant life by walking around in our heavy boots."

Avery bent down, unlaced his boots, and then stepped out onto the grass in his stocking feet. Carefully, he marched past the other scouts in their neon orange safety vests to where their leader, Mr. Marshall, stood in the hot sun, reading a map.

As soon as Mr. Marshall saw Avery approach, he braced himself. *This kid is driving us all nuts*, he thought. He looked down and smiled. "Yes, Avery?"

Avery explained how their work cleaning up the ditch was actually making things worse.

"We're trampling on all the plant life," he complained.

"Hey!" Ben shouted. "Look at this!"

All the other scouts were gathered around a flower in the shade of an elm tree. Avery pushed himself to the center of the group. He looked at what Ben was pointing at and his jaw dropped and his eyes goggled. "A *Dionaea muscipula*," he whispered.

"It's a Venus flytrap," said Ben.

"That's what I said," snapped Avery. "Don't anyone touch it." He bent down to inspect the brilliant pink flower.

"Look at those teeth around the edge," said a scout.

"They're called cilia," said Avery. "Oh, perfect! A spider!"

A small white spider was climbing up the stem of the flytrap. All the boys held their breath as the creature stepped closer to the flower's pink mouth. The spider clambered up the middle of the bloom, avoiding the long, tooth-like fibers on either side. But in less than five seconds, the jaws of the flower snapped shut, trapping the bug.

Avery straightened up. "See, Mr. Marshall? This is exactly what I was talking about.

The plant life here is too important for us to go marching around with our bags and our poking sticks."

"Avery," said Mr. Marshall calmly. "I have a special mission for you."

Several moments later, Avery and two other scouts, Roger and Dante, were stepping around bushes and small trees beyond the ditch. "Mr. Marshall said that sometimes when people throw junk from their cars it can get all the way up here," explained Avery.

Roger leaned over to Dante. "He just wanted to get Avery out of his hair," he whispered.

"So why punish *us*?" asked Dante.

In the first ten minutes, the three boys found pop cans, straws, and crumpled up bags and containers from fast food restaurants. As they walked deeper and deeper into the woods, farther away from the ditch and the highway, they didn't find any more garbage to clean up. The sun was high overhead, and the boys became hot, thirsty, and bored.

"Maybe we'll find another one of those Venus trap things," said Dante.

"I doubt it," said Avery from up ahead. "Those are very rare." Suddenly Avery froze. "Someone else is here."

The other boys walked up beside him. Avery was staring at a big khaki-colored tent. It looked large enough to hold three or four campers, but there was no one inside. The flap was open, and they could see the clean, quiet interior.

"Who'd want to camp out here?" asked Roger.

Dante stepped up to the open flap. "Do you think someone just left it here?" he asked. "Like maybe whoever was camping here, like, died?"

Avery glanced around. "Well, there're no hiking packs or sleeping bags. No garbage, either." He sniffed the air. "But I smell food," he said.

Dante sniffed. "Yeah!" he said. "It smells like chocolate." He cautiously stepped inside. "This tent is nicer than the one Mr. Marshall has," he said.

"It is a nice tent," Avery agreed.

Roger joined Dante inside. "I bet a bunch of us could fit in here," he said. "And the floor is really soft."

The tent flap suddenly snapped shut. The walls of the tent swiftly collapsed on the two boys, trapping them inside.

"The walls are sticky!" shouted Roger. "I can't move!"

The walls folded in on themselves, wrapping tightly around the struggling Roger and Dante. Outside, Avery could see their human forms outlined in the khaki fabric as if they were covered in plastic wrap. Soon their bodies were wrapped so tightly they couldn't move their arms or heads. Then the tent began to shrink.

Avery watched in awe as the khaki-colored mound grew smaller around its captives, dragging them down into the ground. Huge leaves reached out from under the tent and covered the struggling mass. After a few moments, there was no more movement and no sound, except for the buzzing of insects.

Avery hadn't moved the entire time. He didn't even notice the beads of sweat that ran down the sides of his face.

After what seemed like a hundred years, Avery whistled. Then, slowly, he said to himself, "That was the coolest thing ever." He turned and began walking back through the trees and shrubs. "An unknown species, I'll bet. Maybe I can even name it after me."

Avery kept his head down as he walked. *No,* he thought. *Maybe I'll just keep it a secret for now.* Soon, he could just make out the ditch beyond the trunks of the trees. He heard the voices of the other scouts. *Maybe I could show it to someone else,* he thought. *But I'll wait until tomorrow.* He looked up at the sky. *Noon. It should be hungry by then.*

HELLO
DARKNESS

The three girls heard the whimper of the puppies echoing inside the long, dark pipe. They stood at the edge of the park farthest away from the playground and the parking lot. The ground dropped off here and sloped down to a river shimmering in the October sunlight.

"How did they get in there?" asked Caroline.

"Puppies are curious," said Ray. "They probably just wandered in there, and now they're afraid to come out."

"Why would they be afraid?" asked Megan. "If they wandered in, they can wander back out, right?"

The round mouth of the drainpipe poked out of the grassy hillside. The rest of the steel tube traveled horizontally through the ground, back toward the parking lot and the storm drains.

"Maybe something chased them in there," Caroline suggested.

"I think they're just afraid of the dark," said Ray. She squatted down and peered into the mouth of the tunnel for what must have been the tenth time. "It's really dark in there."

The whimpers grew louder, sadder.

"Poor little things," said Caroline for what also must have been the tenth time.

"Well, we either do something or call for help," said Megan. "What's it going to be?"

Ray stared hard at the mouth of the pipe. "I could crawl in there," she said.

The other two girls exchanged glances. "Are you crazy?" said Megan. "It's dark in there!"

"I'm not afraid of the dark," said Ray.

Caroline shuddered. "I don't like closed-in places," she said. "I'd panic if I climbed in there."

"Let's go get help," said Megan.

"If we do that, we might be too late," said Ray.

Ray looked down at her jeans and decided she didn't care if they got dirty or not.

"Caroline," she said, "go grab that rope we saw over by the tennis court. You can use it to help me get back out."

Without a word, Caroline dashed toward the other end of the park. Megan bent over and looked at the pipe. "You don't know how far in they are," she said.

Ray smiled. "It can't be too far. We can still hear them," she said.

Caroline quickly returned with the rope. "When I find them, I'll put them in my backpack," said Ray. "Then you two can pull me out." The girl dropped to her knees. "I'll call for you when I'm ready."

Ray shrugged off her backpack and held it in her hand. "It might be too narrow in there to take it off," she said. Taking a deep breath, Ray turned to the pipe. She squirmed inside. "Wish me luck," came her muffled voice from inside. Her legs quickly disappeared from sight. Before long, the other girls couldn't see the soles of her shoes anymore. The tunnel was too dark.

Both Caroline and Megan were worried about their friend's decision.

After a couple of minutes, Caroline knelt down and yelled, "Are you okay?"

A voice echoed back. "I'm fine. I think I'm getting closer."

The sound of the puppies had died down. Megan and Caroline could hear only a rustling sound that they assumed was their friend.

In a few minutes, Megan called into the pipe. "Ray, what's happening?"

There was no response. "Ray!" she shouted.

The rustling had stopped. The dark tunnel was silent.

Caroline cried, "Ray! Say something!"

A warm breeze ran up the hill from the river below. The grass sighed and the clover flowers danced around them. The two girls watched each other, their expressions worried, as they strained to hear the slightest sound.

A moan echoed from the pipe.

"We're going to get help!" shouted Caroline.

Finally, there was a whisper. "Help."

"Are you okay?" said Caroline. "Do you have the puppies?"

There was a long pause before their friend answered. "There are no puppies," came the whisper.

"What made the sound, then?" Megan asked in a shaky voice.

"It was trying to trick us," Ray whispered from the pipe.

Suddenly, the rope was yanked out of Caroline and Megan's hands. With a sharp snap, the rope lashed back and forth like an angry snake and then disappeared into the drain. The two girls jumped up and screamed.

The sound of the thrashing rope grew fainter and fainter. Then a whisper followed.

"You can't . . . help," came the distant girl's voice. "It's too strong. You have to . . . run . . . run now!"

A thunderous rumble came from inside the pipe. Caroline and Megan turned and ran down the slope.

Neither girl looked back. Neither girl saw the wide, inhuman face filling the space of the tunnel's mouth. A face that licked its slobbering lips and then slid out of the pipe like an enormous shadowy serpent, following the screaming girls as they raced toward the river.

THE BOY
WHO
WAS IT

The sharp slice of moon, curved like a grin, hung above the neighborhood trees. Below, in the uncut grass among the maze of trees, Bennie and his friends ran and hid and screamed.

"You're It!" shouted one.

"Now you're It!" cried another.

Back and forth, the game of hide-and-seek combined with tag had been going for hours. Bennie had only been It once. He was perhaps the fastest runner among his friends. Poor Mateo had been It a dozen times.

Finally, Mateo stopped. "I hate being It."

The group of friends stopped leaping and laughing. They moved in toward Mateo.

"Being It is fun," lied Robert.

"No, it's not," said Mateo. "It's not fair."

"Well, at least you're not really *It*," said Bennie, with a grin.

All his friends, including Mateo, turned to stare at him.

"Not really It?" echoed Mateo. "What does that mean?"

"Yeah. You're not the real It," said Bennie calmly. "The reason this game started in the first place. Where do you think the idea for It came from?"

Sara shook her head. "Are you making this up?" she said.

Bennie put a hand to his chest. "Me? Make things up? I heard this story from my dad."

"So, what is . . . It?" Mateo asked quietly.

"No one's really sure," said Bennie. "Some kind of monster or something. A creature like Bigfoot that lives in these woods. My dad read about It in the paper when he was a kid. This It thing always stayed out of sight behind the trees, just like these ones." Bennie gestured toward the huge elm trees that surrounded them. "He was half-human, half-beast."

"See, Mateo?" said Robert. "Being It is like being a monster. Like, powerful. Mighty."

"Like creepy," said Jess.

"They say the first It was a kid just like us," said Bennie. "A kid who was playing with his friends, then got lost in the woods. Something happened to him. I don't know if he got bit, or was poisoned by plants, or what. But he changed. He got big and hairy. His hands turned into claws. His teeth grew so big he couldn't shut his mouth. He was drooling and hungry all the time."

"Cut it out, Ben!" said Sara.

Bennie tried to look innocent. "I'm just telling you what I heard," he said.

The moon no longer hung overhead. It had sunk below the dark branches of the elms. With the moonlight gone, the woods had grown darker. The friends still stood in a circle around Mateo. Only a siren, far away, broke the silence.

"One more game," said Robert, trying to change the mood. "One more, okay? And Mateo, you're It. So be like a monster when you find us and tag us."

"Okay," said Mateo, shrugging his shoulders.

Mateo shut his eyes and counted to twenty while the other kids scattered. Then he looked up and shouted, "Ready or not, here It comes!" He growled half-heartedly and then disappeared among the trees, looking for his friends.

After a few minutes, another sound echoed through the trees. "Kids! Time to go home!" It was Mr. Lopez, Bennie's dad. He was standing in his backyard, yelling toward the trees. "Time for supper!"

Bennie and his friends slowly marched out of the woods and into the pool of light shining from the Lopez's back door. Robert, Sara, and the others all said their goodbyes to Bennie and his dad, filing around the corner of the house and back to their own homes.

Bennie watched them all leave as he stood at the back door. Something bothered him about their departure, but he wasn't quite sure what.

In the middle of supper, Mrs. Lopez's cell phone buzzed.

"No phones at the table, Mom," Bennie called.

Mrs. Lopez had a serious look on her face as she glanced at her phone. "It's Mrs. Ruiz," she said, getting up with the phone and heading into the kitchen.

Mateo's mom, thought Bennie. And suddenly he knew what had bothered him about his friends leaving after the game. He didn't remember seeing Mateo among them.

Mrs. Lopez returned to the table. "Bennie, was Mateo playing with you tonight?"

Bennie nodded.

"His mom says he hasn't come home," said Mrs. Lopez.

"The kids all left at the same time," said her husband. "Right, Bennie?"

"Uh, yeah, right. But I didn't see Mateo, actually," he said.

"He'll show up," said Mr. Lopez. "Mateo moves a little slower sometimes."

While getting ready for bed later, Bennie stared out his bedroom window toward the wooded lot next door. The trunks of the trees were swallowed in darkness. *Did Mateo get lost somehow?* he wondered.

His phone buzzed. It was Robert. "Did you hear about Mateo?" he said. "Nobody can find him. His parents have been calling everyone."

Bennie couldn't talk. The inside of his mouth felt rough. His tongue felt like cardboard.

"You made up that story, right?" said Robert.

Bennie swallowed hard. "Yeah, yeah, of course. It's just a scary story."

Robert paused. "You don't think that happened to Mateo, do you?" he asked. "Like he got lost or turned into It?"

"It's a story!" said Bennie. "Don't be stupid!" Then he clicked his phone off.

Bennie was unable to sleep that night. He lay in bed staring out of his window, gazing at the dark treetops and the stars beyond.

He heard a growl from outside. He jumped out of bed, ran to the window, and opened the screen. He leaned out into the cool air. There it was again. A growl. And it came from the woods.

A dog, thought Bennie. Then he heard it a third time. It didn't sound like a dog or any other animal he recognized.

Bennie stared hard at the edge of the woods that bordered the Lopez yard. A faint light spilling from the kitchen windows was just enough to see by. Bennie spotted a shape, something moving between the trees. Something big.

Bennie kept staring, but eventually it stopped moving and he lost sight of the shape in the darkness. He slowly returned to his bed.

While he lay there, Bennie heard another growl. This time he didn't want to get up and look out the window. This growl sounded louder. Closer.

Then he heard something that sounded like the back door opening. He kept his head on his pillow, but his ears were alert and straining to hear. A muffle. A thud. Was something coming up the stairs? *I must be dreaming,* he thought.

A low growl came from just outside his closed door. A groan. The door handle twitched, and the door slowly opened. In the dim glow of the hall nightlight, Bennie saw the silhouette of a huge and hairy beast. Its long arms reached down to the floor. The face was hidden in the darkness, but Bennie thought he could see two spots of red where its eyes should've been. A strand of drool gleamed in the dim light.

Bennie couldn't move. His body was frozen to the bed. As the hairy body drew nearer he smelled something unpleasant, like food left in the refrigerator too long.

Bennie couldn't help watching the beast as it lumbered closer and closer.

He tried lifting his head. "Mateo," he whispered. "Mateo . . . is that you?"

A low growl shook the bedroom. The tall creature bent over the frightened boy. A hairy paw reached out toward the covers.

Then Bennie saw the beast's toothy mouth form words. "Tag. You're It!"

WHY DAD DESTROYED THE SANDBOX

We used to have a sandbox in our yard, but had to get rid of it. My dad destroyed it, actually.

My family just moved into town two weeks ago. We bought a huge old house, out past the lake. It's three stories, and my little sister and I each have our own room. I even have a separate room for my books and a TV for watching movies.

The area is perfect for our two golden labs, Achilles and Hector. They have lots of room to run around. We have woods in the back, a little cement building called a sauna, a blueberry bog, a couple tire swings, and we used to have a huge sandbox. I mean, huge. It could hold twenty people at once. Well, twenty kids, I mean.

When we first moved in, the sandbox was empty. I figured the people who had lived there before us must have been super greedy. They took the sand with them when they moved! My dad bought a dozen bags of sand and filled it up.

Unfortunately for me, my little sister, Linda, loved it. The sandbox sat behind a line of evergreen trees, and my mom couldn't see it from the house, so she worried that Linda might get lost or something. Every time she wanted to play in the sandbox, I had to babysit. I would bring a book with me and sit on the low, wooden bench that lined the box.

After the first week, something odd happened with the sandbox. One morning, Linda and I tromped out there and suddenly she stopped and shouted, "Someone stole my sand!" The sandbox was empty.

When my dad came out to look, he stood there and rubbed his nose. "Where did it go?" he said.

"Burglars stole it!" cried Linda.

"Yeah, right," I said.

Dad knelt down, stared under the bench, and felt the sides of the box. "Must have leaked out."

"Sand burglars!" shouted Linda.

Dad said not to worry, he'd buy more sand and fill up the box.

Three days later, the sandbox was empty again. Dad nailed more boards to the floor and around the sides. He refilled it. And Linda went back to playing in it. She kept talking about treasures in the sand. Once she found a man's old-fashioned watch in the sandbox, and another time an old doll. I figured she just put them in there herself. We were always finding weird junk lying around the property of that big place. For a while, everything seemed to be normal.

Then one day Aunt Dotty and Uncle Bob came by to visit. They brought my cousins, Mandy and Kyle. Kyle was my age so we usually hung out together. But my mom said the dreaded words: "Why don't you take Mandy out to see your sandbox?" What she was really saying was, "Robin, would you watch the little kids while they have fun? You don't mind being bored, do you?"

"Fine," I said. What else could I say?

We showed Kyle and Mandy the giant sandbox. "That thing is huge!" said Kyle. See, I told you.

Linda and Mandy jumped inside and started playing. Meanwhile, Kyle and I walked around. I showed him the rest of the place, always keeping an eye on the sandbox. Kyle and I both like *Turok, Son of Stone* comic books. I had the newest one, so I told Kyle to wait with the little kids while I ran inside to grab it.

I had just picked up the comic from my bed when I heard the scream. I ran downstairs. Kyle was standing inside the doorway, panting, his face white. "Mandy," he stuttered. "Mandy . . ."

All of us ran outside to the sandbox. Linda was standing on the bench, crying and pointing. Inside the box was a circular, cone-shaped dent in the sand. "Mandy's gone!" screamed Linda.

Aunt Dotty shouted and ran into the box. Uncle Bob and Dad pulled her back. Then Dad carefully crawled into the remaining sand. He started digging through the sand, where Mandy had vanished. He dug deeper until he reached the wooden bottom. Some sand was sifting into the cracks between the boards.

"Get back!" yelled Dad. He hurried out of the sandbox. Then he and Uncle Bob grabbed one side of the box and lifted it. It must have been really heavy because they were both grunting and sweating. When the sandbox was removed, we all just stared. I couldn't believe it. There was nothing there. No hole, no tunnel — nothing. Just bare dirt.

Aunt Dotty knelt down and clawed at the dirt. "Mandy!" she screamed into the ground. Uncle Bob grabbed her shoulders and pulled her to her feet. Mom said, "Let's get the kids inside, and we'll call the fire department." We all turned to go, but then Aunt Dotty made a weird sound.

"That's Mandy's," she said, pointing. We looked at the sandbox in its new position, and saw a bright pink ribbon sitting on top of the sand.

"How did that get there?" asked Uncle Bob. Aunt Dotty stepped into the sandbox to retrieve the ribbon and suddenly, she sank down to her armpits. "Bob!" she shouted. "Help me!"

Uncle Bob ran toward her, but it was too late. She sank out of sight with a scream. We could hear her voice dying away as she fell. Uncle Bob and Dad lifted the sandbox a second time and searched, but there was no hole.

The fire department came and examined the ground around the sandbox. After a couple hours they told Uncle Bob they didn't find anything. They told us that the whole town was built on sand. One of the firemen suggested they fell into some kind of sinkhole. But how could they sink through the sandbox with all the bottom boards still in place? And why couldn't we find a hole?

I guess Linda and I were just lucky all this time.

Dad chopped up the sandbox with an axe. Then he built a fence between that area and the house. He didn't want the dogs running around over there. But a couple days later, I was calling the dogs and Hector never showed up.

I know we just moved into that house, but now Mom and Dad want to move. I don't want to leave until we've found Hector. I plan to go out every day after school and hunt for him. So if I don't show up to class some day, I might've sunk into the ground too. Or we might have moved. Just to let you know.

SECTION 2

DON'T TURN OFF THE LIGHT!

THE DRAIN

Arjun hated drains. He couldn't watch the soapy water flowing past his bare feet and swirling into the shower drain. If things went *down* a drain, that meant that things could also come *up*. Anything.

A flash of lightning lit up the bathroom and shower stall. Then darkness.

"This is just great!" Arjun said aloud to himself. "Just great!"

He carefully climbed out of the shower, feeling his way through utter darkness to the towel rack. "That's all we need," he said. "Another power outage!"

Arjun dried off, got dressed, and then groped his way into the living room where he found his father hunched over a glowing blue light.

"Dad, how can you still be playing games?" he asked. "There's a storm outside and the power's out. It's all over the neighborhood. No lights. Nothing."

"Huh, that's cool," his dad mumbled without taking his eyes off his handheld device.

Arjun was always worried about losing power. Everything in his world — everything important that is — relied on a constant supply of power. How could he live without batteries, chargers, wall outlets, or wireless Internet?

The boy walked over behind his dad.

"Uh, oh. Look at your battery icon," Arjun said, peering over his dad's right shoulder. "You're running on reserves and they're almost gone."

From where he stood, he could see the blue screen of the handheld device.

His dad never took his eyes off the glowing screen in his hands. "It's fine, Ari," he said. "No worries. I'll be able to finish this game long before —"

His dad stopped talking. There was a low hum, and Arjun's father slumped over in his chair. The handheld device dropped from his grasp and slid onto the floor. He looked once more at the battery indicator built into his dad's back.

No power.

"Great!" said Arjun, rolling his eyes. "Another power drain." Arjun hated drains.

Maybe having a robot father is just too much work, he thought. Maybe he should ask for a refund.

BUMP IN THE NIGHT

Violet got a Skype alert in the middle of the night. After she got out of bed and walked over to her computer, she let out a groan. Why was Jane calling her? Her little sister was supposed to be sleeping over at a friend's house. And why wasn't she using her phone?

Violet clicked the "accept call" button. As soon as little Jane's face came onto the screen, Violet snapped, "Why are you bugging me?"

Jane looked upset. "Violet, you have to come over here now!" she cried. "You have to come help me!"

Violet was a little bit concerned, but she

figured her little sister was just homesick. "You'll be fine, Janey. I'm going back to bed."

"But something bad is happening. Really bad," Jane said. "You know how Victoria said her house was haunted by a bump in the night? Well, it is! And it's a big bump!"

"Old houses make weird noises at night," Violet said matter-of-factly.

"No," said Jane. "I don't mean a bump like a noise. I mean, a *bump*! Like a lump. A lump of something under the rug."

"Hah!" Violet said. "Did you have too much candy tonight? You must be dreaming."

"No, I mean it!" Jane shouted. "We were watching a scary movie —"

"See?" interrupted Violet. "You're having a nightmare."

"I'm telling the truth, Vi," Jane said seriously. "We saw part of the living room rug start to rise, like something was underneath it. Like when the cat gets under the bed sheets, you know? And then Victoria's dad yelled, 'It's here again!' And everyone in the house ran to their rooms."

"So then where's Victoria?" asked Violet.

"I don't know!" said Jane. "The bump was chasing us, moving under the rug really fast.

When we got to the hall, there was no rug.
The bump kept coming, only it was under
the wood floor this time. We ran up this big
old staircase, and it kept following us. Then
somehow it slid up the wall and was moving
under the wallpaper! It never stopped. I made
it to Victoria's bedroom, and she was supposed
to be right behind me. That's when I heard
her scream."

"Who scream?" Violet asked, sounding bored.

"Victoria!" Jane yelled. She was sounding
more and more panicked. "Aren't you listening
to me? She's gone! I'm locked in her room. I'm
using her computer, because I left my phone
downstairs. I'm thinking if the bump can move
under wood or wallpaper, it must be able to
squeeze under a door . . . oh, no, look!"

Jane must have turned Victoria's computer
camera in a different direction, because now
Violet was looking at another part of Victoria's
bedroom.

"Do you see it, Vi? Do you see it?" Jane asked.

Violet's screen was dim. It was hard to see
anything. She thought she saw a dark shape
next to a door, but she couldn't be sure. She
shook her head slowly.

"It's the bump! It's here! It's in the room!"
Jane yelled.

Violet's computer screen went blank. The Skype session ended. Violet sat back in her chair and stared.

This was a prank, she decided. Jane and Victoria were pranking her. Or else her little sister was having a nightmare. A bump in the night? How stupid was that?

Pop!

Something next to the wall sizzled and sparkled. Violet saw tiny sparks fizzing out of the plug where her computer cord was attached to the outlet. *It must be short-circuiting,* she thought. Then, slowly, the cord next to the wall expanded like a balloon.

It was the bump.

The bump traveled along the cord. It moved closer to the computer sitting on Violet's desk.

Violet jumped up from her chair and stood, watching, unable to move, unable to believe what she was seeing.

The bump inside the cord moved closer and closer. It reached the computer. Then it disappeared. The cord was back to its normal size.

What is going on? thought Violet.

Now the computer was expanding. The keyboard stretched up and out. The screen grew larger and rounder. White shapes that looked like teeth formed around the edge of the screen. They grew longer and sharper as the computer grew larger.

Violet stepped back.

The bump that used to be a computer grew so large it forced the girl into a corner of her bedroom. She couldn't move. The last thing she saw was Jane staring out at her from deep inside the computer screen with wide, frightened eyes.

THE RACK

Walter saw things out of the corners of his eyes. His older brother sneaking up to scare him, for instance. His science teacher, Mr. Hayes, walking toward his desk when Walter was reading the latest Iron Man comic. Annoying runners on the sidewalk when he was walking to the comic book store. These were all things it was helpful to see, to know in advance, so he could prepare himself. Turn to yell at his brother. Hide Iron Man under his science book. Step aside so the huffing, puffing runner wouldn't knock him over.

But Walter saw other things too. Things he couldn't always explain. Not at first.

Once, he thought he saw an ogre-like being squatting in the corner of his grandmother's living room. He turned and saw that it was just a fancy, old-fashioned chair with a quilt draped over it. At the grocery store he was sure he saw a tall werewolf peering over his shoulder. It turned out to be a large cardboard cutout of a cartoon character for cereal.

"Walter, you're so stupid," he told himself. "Calm down and take a look before you think an alien from another planet is going to attack you or something."

Walter's family lived in a small, crowded house, so there were lots of weird shapes he saw from the corners of his eyes. It always turned out to be a shadow, or light from a car outside a window, or wind blowing the curtains. Or his cat, Fido.

The shape that bothered him most was the coatrack in the back hallway. It stood seven feet tall and was made out of dark wood with six claw feet. At the top were six short branches, where anyone could hang a coat or hat or scarf. Every time Walter walked past the hallway, even though he knew it was the same old coatrack, he thought he saw a man standing there. Out of the corner of his eye he saw a tall, skinny man without a face. Of course he didn't have a face, Walter told himself. There was no face. It was just his dad's hat. A long coat had suggested a tall, slender body. All the same, Walter never walked down that hallway at night.

One afternoon, he came home after school and the house felt empty. Again, like a hundred other times, he saw the skinny man out of the corner of his eye. Tall and slender. Long dark arms scraping against the floor. No face. This time, however, Walter was prepared.

"Don't be so dramatic," he whispered to himself. "Don't freak out. It's the same dumb coatrack that's always there." Walter refused to turn and look at the coatrack, proving to himself that he was not stupid. Not afraid.

Walter heard a noise. He had thought the house was empty.

"Is that you, honey?" came his mother's voice from somewhere upstairs.

Walter felt the tension melt away from his shoulders. "Yeah, I'm home," he replied.

"I've been busy cleaning all day," said his mother. "So don't walk on the kitchen floor until it's dry."

"Okay, Mom."

"And if you're wondering where that old coatrack is," she added, "I moved it out of the back hallway. It's by the front door now."

Walter felt as if he had fallen into a pool of ice-cold water.

There was no coatrack in the hallway.

He couldn't move. He couldn't make himself turn around to look.

Something behind him cleared its throat. Then he heard the sound of knuckles scraping against the floor.

SCARING
VINNY

"Vinny! Stop scaring your little brother!"

"But he likes it!"

"No, I don't," said Vinny's little brother, Stevie.

Vinny laughed. "Yes, you do," he said. "You love being scared."

"I said stop," Vinny's mother repeated.

Vinny rolled his eyes. "This is Halloween week," he said. "Everyone is supposed to scare each other. It's funny."

"It's not funny," Stevie said.

"You always laugh after I scare you," Vinny pointed out.

"I don't like that story about the ghosts under the bed," said Stevie quietly.

"They were gremlins," said Vinny. "Not ghosts."

"And no jumping out and shouting, 'Boo,'" said their mother. "No more fake spiders or rubber snakes. No more pointing out the window and saying you saw a monster."

Vinny half-listened to her. "Whatever," he said.

His mother sighed and looked up at the living room clock. "You two need to think about getting to bed."

Vinny rushed out of the living room first. He had a plan. He didn't care what his mother had said; scaring people was fun. Especially around Halloween time. And no matter if Stevie screamed or cried, he always joked about being scared when it was all over.

Vinny ran to Stevie's room. Something his little brother said had given him an idea. He would hide under the bed. Then, when it got quiet, Vinny would reach around with a claw-like hand and growl. It would be perfect!

Hmm. Should he growl like a werewolf or more like an ogre?

Vinny ran quickly to Stevie's bed and slipped

underneath. He held his breath and waited. He heard footsteps coming down the hall. Then he heard the snap of the light switch.

With light illuminating the underside of Stevie's bed, Vinny saw that he was not alone. Next to him lay a small collection of furry dust balls. Dust balls with eyes and tiny teeth. But they weren't actually dust balls. They were gremlins! They hopped up and down excitedly, without making a sound. The largest one, with a long tongue and spiky hair, jumped up on Vinny's shoulder. It hopped close to his face and then glowered into the boy's eyes, grinning.

"Let's all scare him together," whispered the gremlin. "Won't that be fun?"

SPOT ON THE CEILING

Mrs. Lunder did not care for dogs of any kind. It didn't matter what breed or size or color. It didn't matter if it was big, small, hairy, sleek, noisy, or quiet. A dog was a dog, and she would never let her son, Donnie, bring one into the house.

"Please, please can I have a dog?" Donnie asked for the thousandth time. It was evening, and he and his parents were sitting in what his mother called their "together" room. Mrs. Lunder sat doing embroidery and Mr. Lunder was playing a game on his phone while Donnie read a comic book. Every few minutes he'd put the comic on his lap and ask, "But why? Why can't I have a dog? A puppy?"

"You know the answer," said Mr. Lunder.

"Paulie got a new puppy," said Donnie. Paulie was his friend down the block. "She's really, really cute. Her name is Tulip."

Mrs. Lunder squinted at her embroidery hoop. She stabbed it with a needle and pulled a long green thread through the fabric. "No dogs," she said. "Dogs drool."

"Tulip doesn't drool," said Donnie.

"They leave hair everywhere," said his mother.

"We could get a hairless dog," said Donnie.

She grunted. "Hairless dogs are the worst kind."

"Please?" begged Donnie. "I'll take good care of her."

Mr. Lunder chuckled. "The same way you took care of your pet turtle?"

Donnie had stepped on his pet turtle months ago and crushed its shell. "It was an accident," he mumbled.

"The same way you took care of all those dead goldfish?" said Mrs. Lunder. "Or the lovebird you let out of its cage?"

"You don't have a very good track record," said Mr. Lunder.

"No dogs," repeated Mrs. Lunder, ending the conversation.

That night in bed, Donnie closed his eyes and thought of how Tulip had jumped up on his lap over at Paulie's house. He remembered how good the puppy smelled, how soft its black fur felt beneath his fingers.

Donnie stared up at the ceiling, a frown on his face. His parents were being mean and selfish.

Donnie noticed a spot on the ceiling. It must have been an old stain, but he'd never noticed it till now. Maybe it was only because he was thinking so hard about Tulip, but the stain reminded him of a dog. A soft outline resembled a jumping puppy. A crack in the plaster lay where the puppy's mouth would have been.

Donnie frowned deeper. *The only dog I'll ever have,* he thought. *A stain on the ceiling.* Then his frown softened. A smile touched his lips. *Well, it's something,* he told himself. *Better than nothing. Ha! I'll call him Spot. The perfect name.*

The boy fell asleep, dreaming of Spot crawling into his lap and licking his face.

Over the next few weeks, Donnie would stare up at the stain on the ceiling every night and imagine all sorts of adventures for him and Spot. They would race together, they'd explore the woods on the other side of town, they'd visit Paulie, and Tulip and Spot would become great friends. He and Paulie could train them to catch balls in the backyard or flying plastic discs at the park.

Mr. and Mrs. Lunder did not notice that Donnie had stopped asking for a dog. The subject never came up. And his parents never thought of bringing it up. Then one night, at dinner, Donnie said, "Spot and I found a dead raccoon in the woods today."

"Dead raccoon?" squealed Mrs. Lunder. She dropped her spoon into the soup.

"Who's Spot?" asked Mr. Lunder.

"My dog," said Donnie cheerfully, sipping his soup.

"You don't have a dog," Mrs. Lunder said.

Donnie shrugged. "Well, he's not like other dogs."

"Do you mean he's imaginary?" asked his father.

Donnie nodded. "And he doesn't drool or leave hair anywhere or jump on the furniture."

Mrs. Lunder wiped her mouth with a napkin, then folded it carefully on her lap. "I forbid it."

"What?" asked her husband.

"We said no dogs," said Mrs. Lunder. "And no dogs means no dogs."

"But —" Donnie started.

"I don't care for any dogs in this house," said Mrs. Lunder. "I have been crystal clear. And you went ahead and defied me by making up this . . . this unreal creature."

"It doesn't hurt anything," said Donnie.

"I said no, and I meant it," said Mrs. Lunder.

Mr. Lunder cleared his throat. "Where is this dog, Donnie?" he asked gently.

Donnie kept his eyes on his plate. "In my room," he said. "Above my bed."

Mrs. Lunder sputtered. "Above your —" She stood up and strode toward the boy's bedroom. Donnie and his dad followed quickly.

"Where is it?" Mrs. Lunder bellowed, pushing the door open. "Where?"

Donnie pointed at the ceiling. His parents stared long and hard at the unusual stain. "Oh, it's like looking up at clouds," said Mr. Lunder. "I can sort of see where you might —"

"This is ridiculous," said his mother. "A stain?"

Mr. Lunder was about to speak when his wife cut him off. "This is going against my rule," she said. "This imaginary dog — this stain — is a sign of rebellion. Donnie, you're being deliberately disrespectful." Mrs. Lunder did not like being disobeyed. She stood silent for a moment, and then walked off, returning to the dinner table.

Donnie gazed up at the stain. When his father quietly left the room, Donnie turned and shouted down the hall, "I'm not being anything!" He slammed the bedroom door.

After dinner, Mr. and Mrs. Lunder went into their together room. Mrs. Lunder stabbed at the embroidery fabric as if she were trying to kill a wild animal. Mr. Lunder played his games, but he kept losing points.

"What was that?" asked Mrs. Lunder. She and her husband looked up.

"I don't hear anything," said Mr. Lunder.

A bark broke the silence.

"It's coming from Donnie's room," said Mr. Lunder.

The two grown-ups hurried down the hall back to their son's bedroom. Mr. Lunder grabbed the knob and pushed it open.

"Donnie!" Mrs. Lunder yelled.

The boy was not there. His bed sheets were rumpled as if he had been lying there only a moment before. His slippers lay on the floor. The window was closed and locked against the cold night air.

"Donnie!" yelled his father. "Where are you?"

Another bark echoed through the room. It sounded further away. Mr. Lunder threw open the window and stuck his head out. "Donnie, are you there?" The bark sounded again, softer and more distant. But it was not coming from outside.

Mrs. Lunder wept. Mr. Lunder listened carefully to the bark and then looked up at the ceiling.

"Look!" he cried.

The stain was larger now. It had changed and grown. Now it looked as if the dog were running alongside its master — a small, smiling, and happy boy.

THE CREEPING WOMAN

That evening after Christmas Eve dinner, the Hamilton family celebrated a tradition that eleven-year old Jawan always looked forward to. They told scary stories before they went to bed, before the long, deep night when Santa Claus would bring their gifts.

Five-year old Reesha didn't seem to mind the spooky tales of ghosts and zombies and bumps in the night. All she could think of was presents. She stared at their small fireplace, worried that Santa wouldn't fit down the chimney.

"Santa will find a way in," Mrs. Hamilton reassured her. "He always does."

"Don't worry, Reesha," Jawan said. "Santa is magic. He'll figure out how to get in using the fireplace, no matter what size it is."

"Fireplaces remind me of another story," said Mr. Hamilton. He made everyone gasp with his whispered tale about a phantom face that could be seen in a roaring fire. At the end of the story, he shouted out a loud "Boo!" and grabbed Reesha. Everyone screamed and then laughed. Then the Hamilton children all got ready for bed. Jawan and his brother Drew were walking up the stairs to their bedroom when Shonda, their older sister, hurried past them.

"You better look out for the Creeping Woman," she said.

"What's that?" asked Jawan.

"You haven't heard about her?" Shonda asked, surprised.

"It's just one of those things," said Drew. "You know, a legend."

"It may be a legend," said Shonda, "but it's true. I even heard it on the news tonight."

"You did not!" said Drew.

"Ask Dad," said his sister. She turned her attention to Jawan. "A woman has been seen creeping around houses at night. Sometimes she walks hunched over, like her back is broken. And sometimes she walks on all fours. Like a dog or coyote."

"In the snow?" cried Drew.

"Why does she do that?" asked Jawan, his eyes wide and his skin prickling with fear.

"I don't know," said Shonda. "Maybe to steal Christmas presents?"

"Yeah, right," Drew said. "Or to eat people. Ha!"

"It was on the news," said Shonda. "The creeping woman is out there in the dark." She grinned at them and then scurried to her room and shut the door.

Drew rolled his eyes. "She's a big fat liar," he said to his brother. "It's just another scary story."

"You don't think there's a real woman out there?" asked Jawan.

"Nah, and if there is, we'll just run away," said Drew. "She can't move fast if she's crawling around. And no one's getting my presents!"

The boys settled down in their beds, one on either side of the small room.

Jawan frowned. He sat up and looked at the bedroom door. "Is the front door locked?" he asked.

Drew yawned. "Dad always locks it. Stop worrying."

Jawan lay back down and turned to stare out the window. A streetlight illuminated the falling snow, turning it to glittering diamonds streaming past the window. *There couldn't be a woman crawling out in the snow*, thought Jawan. *She'd be frozen.* He thought about the front door again. Had his father locked it? What about the door to the garage? Maybe he should get up and check. But as Jawan continued to watch the sparkling snow, his bed grew warmer and more comfortable, and soon he fell asleep.

Jawan wasn't the only member of the family worried about doors. Little Reesha thought about them too. She was still worried that Santa might not be able to come inside and leave her presents. After the lights were turned out and everyone had gone to sleep, the little girl crept down the carpeted stairs. Reesha made her way through the living room. She tiptoed past the Christmas tree, past the fireplace, past the coatrack, and walked to the front door.

"Santa can come this way," she said to herself.

She reached for the doorknob, but before she unlocked it, she heard a sound. Something was scratching on the outside of the door.

Reesha smiled. "Santa!" she whispered.

The little girl unlocked the door and pulled it open. She watched, frozen, as an arm reached around the bottom of the door and a woman crawled inside the house. A woman with long, snow-white hair and diamond-bright eyes that glittered with hunger.

THE
FURNACE
MAN

Our house had an old coal furnace in the basement. During the winter, Dad would march downstairs every night after dinner, open the furnace's big metal mouth, and shovel coal inside. Mom kept asking him to buy a new one, but Dad liked shoveling coal. He said it was good exercise and made him feel like our hardy ancestors who worked year round just to survive. He called them "stouthearted."

"You better watch your own heart," Mom would say. "That coal's too heavy."

"Only one shovelful at a time," he'd say.

When the furnace made weird sounds at night, or the when the hot air began to sigh through the heat vents, it scared us kids.

Dad said it was just the Old Man in the Furnace. The weird sounds were just the Old Man waking up, and the sighing was his laughter drifting up on the warm air. Dad thought his talk about the Old Man was funny. But it just made us more frightened.

When he went down to the basement after dinner, Dad said he was going to go "wrestle with the Old Man." Mom rolled her eyes and said to cut it out. My brothers and I would stare at each other and worry. Was Dad really wrestling something down there in the dark? Was that why he was so sweaty and out of breath when he came back up? Or was it from all the shoveling?

A few times we went downstairs with him. He wanted to show us how the furnace worked, in case we had to do it ourselves if he was away from home.

Above the furnace door was a round glass window like a porthole on a ship. When Dad shoveled the coal inside, we could see the inside of the furnace get brighter and brighter. The light would change from dull red to orange to yellow. Once I saw some green and blue flames. "That's from copper mixed in with the coal," Dad explained. "The Old Man must be in a good mood."

One night, Dad took longer than usual in the basement. Mom called down the steps, but he didn't answer. We all ran down and found Dad lying on the floor, the shovel in his hand. He was still breathing.

"It's his heart," said Mom. "Quick, call for help."

My older brothers ran back up the steps to call an ambulance. Mom and I stayed with Dad. She held his hand and bent her head over his chest. I could hear her quietly moaning. Then I heard another sound.

Tap . . . tap . . .

Something was knocking against the round glass window of the furnace. I walked over and looked inside. A man's face stared back at me. His skin was rough like coal, and he was grinning from ear to ear.

"Looks like I won," the man whispered. Mom screamed, and the furnace snapped on, the heat rushing through the house, the sound of laughter spreading through each room.

ZOMBIE

CUPCAKES

Everything about Old Mrs. Heeley was odd. Her clothes were odd and old-fashioned. Her gray hair was squeezed into a lacey hairnet, her plastic glasses hung from a chain around her neck, and she wore mismatched shoes that gave her a limp when she walked.

Mr. and Mrs. Harper had lined up a different babysitter for that evening, but the sitter had come down with the flu. After several more phone calls, the only person available was Mrs. Heeley. She said she'd love to help out. She loved sweet young children.

Thankfully, there was something about the old woman that Kareem and Amina both liked. She brought a tray of homemade cupcakes with her.

The cupcakes were fresh. They smelled of chocolate and raspberry, of lemon and red velvet cake.

"They're my favorite thing to bake," Mrs. Heeley had said when she arrived. She passed the tray to Mr. Harper and smiled at the children. "And I know sweet children like sweet things to eat."

"Right you are, Mrs. Heeley," Mr. Harper said. "And thank you. I'll just put them in the breadbox so they don't get stale."

Soon, Mr. and Mrs. Harper left.

Mrs. Heeley had insisted that the kids wait until after dinner to eat the cupcakes. But when dinner was over, she suggested that the children relax a while in front of the TV.

"What *is* that show you two are watching?" asked Mrs. Heeley.

Amina waved her hand. "It's just about zombies," she said.

"Zombies!" said Mrs. Heeley, startled. "That doesn't sound like a good show for children," said the old woman.

"It's okay," said Kareem. "Our parents let us watch it."

"Zombies aren't real," explained Amina. "It's all pretend."

"Pretend . . ." echoed Mrs. Heeley.

"Amina doesn't have to worry about becoming a zombie," said Kareem. "Zombies like to eat brains, and Amina doesn't have any!"

"Hmm, eating brains doesn't sound very tempting," said Mrs. Heeley.

"Hey, look!" cried Kareem. "There's a zombie eating brains now."

The two children stared at the screen, while Mrs. Heeley returned to her crossword puzzle, tsk-tsking under her breath.

"That reminds me," said Kareem. "Can we have cupcakes now?"

"Please?" begged Amina.

"Yes, I think it's time," Mrs. Heeley said.

Kareem raced into the kitchen ahead of Amina and opened the breadbox. He froze. "What's wrong with the cupcakes?" he whispered.

Crumbs and clumps of cake were scattered throughout the box and all over the kitchen counter. Quickly, he counted. Eight cupcakes. Eight! Mrs. Heeley had brought over sixteen. Four for each member of the Harper family. What had happened?

He peered at the remains of the cupcakes. They looked torn in half. The insides, the wonderful fillings that had smelled so delicious, were gone. As if they had been scooped out.

"What did you do to the cupcakes?" yelled Amina. She walked up behind Kareem. "You ruined them!"

"I didn't do it," said Kareem.

"Only two at the most," called Mrs. Heeley from the other room. "Save the rest for tomorrow."

"Something's wrong with them!" cried Amina.

"Wrong?"

Old Mrs. Heeley limped into the kitchen and made her way to the counter. She stared at the breadbox.

"What did you children do?" she exclaimed.

"Nothing," said Kareem. He explained that the mess was exactly how it looked when he opened the breadbox.

"Well," said Mrs. Heeley, "cupcakes don't just fall apart like that. Or disappear. I know you did something."

"Maybe zombies got them," said Amina.

"Or maybe some children snuck in here while I wasn't watching," said the old woman.

Kareem and Amina protested, but Mrs. Heeley was having none of it. She said it was time for bed and no arguing.

But before they left the kitchen, and while the woman's back was turned, Kareem grabbed a cupcake with thick chocolate frosting. In his bedroom he bit into the dark cake and his tongue discovered a creamy glob of tart raspberry jam. It was delicious.

Lying in bed later that night, Kareem gazed at the shadows of tree branches on his bedroom ceiling. The image of the torn cupcakes kept spinning through his brain. Did mice get into the cupcakes? A hungry robber? Aliens? Ghosts?

Kareem heard a noise. He climbed out of bed and cracked open his door. Something, or someone, was moving through the house. He heard a faint *ping*, then another. Whatever it was, the sounds were coming from the kitchen.

Kareem snuck down the hallway. Mrs. Harper left the small light above the oven on every night, so Kareem could see clearly enough in the dim, empty room. He could hear Mrs. Heeley snoring in the living room, and he was careful not to make a sound.

Scritch, scratch . . .

The noise was coming from the breadbox.

So it was *mice!* Kareem hated mice. He grabbed a wooden spoon from a nearby holder and held it over his head. With his other hand, he slowly reached for the plastic knob on the breadbox lid. With a flick of his hand, he flipped it open.

No tails. No whiskers. Nothing squeaking. But there was movement. The cupcakes were on their sides, rocking back and forth ever so slightly. It was as if someone had shaken the breadbox and then suddenly stopped. Kareem counted them. Only five full cupcakes. More of them were torn apart and their soft insides had been scooped out.

Kareem picked up one of the full cakes. It looked puffier than before. Bigger. The frosting was brighter, too, with three different colors of icing mixed together.

"I knew it was you!" Kareem spun around and saw his sister watching him.

"No, no," said Kareem. "I just got here. Look." He held out the cupcake to her. "Does this look bigger to you?"

"Bigger?" Amina made a face. "You mean fatter? I don't know. Hey, what happened to the other ones?"

Kareem shrugged. The brother and sister stood side by side, surveying the breadbox and the cakey mess.

"The fat ones *are* fatter, I think," said Amina. "Do you think they've been eating up the other ones?"

Kareem was about to laugh, but his eye caught a glimpse of the torn apart cakes again. The insides were gone. Licked clean. The way a zombie ate brains.

"Okay, this is nuts!" said Kareem. "You've been eating them!"

"I didn't do it," said Amina, pouting. "You did it, and you're trying to blame me."

Kareem shook his head. "I'm going to bed. And so are you. We'll figure this out in the morning."

Amina didn't argue. She closed the breadbox and followed her brother out of the kitchen.

Before she walked down the hall to her bedroom, Amina stopped. "If they are zombie cupcakes," she whispered, "think what would have happened if we ate one."

"What do you mean?" said Kareem, worried.

Amina shuddered. "We would have turned into one of them. The living dead!" she said.

Kareem shook his head. "I eat French fries all the time," he said. "Do I look like a French fry? Have any French fries eaten me? Go to bed, Amina."

Kareem watched her go into her bedroom and shut the door. He was still worried. He raced back to the kitchen, convinced it was mice or some other animal. And he would wait all night until he caught them.

As he entered the kitchen, he heard a squeak. A tiny cry of pain. The sound sent goose bumps up and down his neck. He opened the breadbox and saw only two cupcakes left. More crumbs were scattered around them. But no frosting. He hadn't realized that the first time. No blobs of sugary icing or creamy insides. Only cake crumbs. So where did the frosting go?

Carefully, Kareem picked up the two remaining cupcakes. He hurried back to his room and set them on top of his dresser. He planned to watch them all night.

If a human ate a zombie cupcake, what would happen to them? Would they become a zombie too? Is that a new way for someone to become a member of the living dead? *I only ate one,* he thought. *Only one.*

As it grew late, Kareem's eyes drooped and he started dreaming. Cupcakes and zombies . . .

The next morning, Kareem jumped out of bed and ran to his mirror. He looked the same. No signs of cake or frosting. He was still human. He laughed at how scared he had felt. Then he checked his dresser.

The cupcakes were gone.

Kareem rushed to the kitchen. He was going to tell his parents what had happened the night before, but when he walked through the kitchen doorway, he was startled to find Old Mrs. Heeley hunched over the stove.

"Oh, hi, sweetie," she said.

Kareem was confused. "Where are Mom and Dad?" he asked.

Mrs. Heeley wiped her hands on a towel hanging from the stove. "Well, your dad's at work," she said. "And your mom forgot she had to see the dentist. She called me early this morning and asked me to walk over and keep an eye on you two." The old woman giggled. "As if you two big kids need a babysitter."

"Hey, wait a minute. Today's Saturday," said Kareem. "Dad doesn't work on Saturdays."

"I'm sure that's what your mother told me," said Mrs. Heeley.

"Morning," said Amina cheerfully, bouncing into the kitchen.

"Good morning, little one," said Mrs. Heeley.

Amina whispered to Kareem, "So did you enjoy eating all the cupcakes when no one was around?"

Kareem leaned toward her and said, "Disappointed I'm not a zombie?"

Amina glared at him. "You haven't eaten enough," she said. "You have to eat a lot before you change."

Kareem looked at the stout old woman in front of the stove. *I'll bet she's eaten a lot of them,* he thought. *She said they were her favorite thing to bake.*

"Why don't you go into the dining room and I'll finish making your breakfast. How does that sound?" Mrs. Heeley said.

"Great!" said Amina.

"And I'll add a few of my special ingredients," she said.

Kareem stared at her. The old woman patted his head. Kareem turned and headed into the dining room to join his sister.

"So sweet," the old woman said. She licked her lips greedily. Under her breath she mumbled, "And both of them so smart. I wonder how sweet their little brains taste?"

SECTION 3

DON'T BLINK

THE
ELEVATOR
GAME

It was after school, and Leo and Sam were riding the city bus home. Their families lived in apartments downtown, so they didn't take the regular school buses like everyone else did. The city bus was always crowded, and it stopped at every block. By the time the boys got home, it was usually dark.

"Have you heard of the elevator game?" Sam asked.

"Is that the one with the spooky lady?" asked Leo.

"Yeah," said Sam. He lowered his voice. "They say a woman fell down an elevator shaft and died. Her ghost is all bloody, and she haunts anyone who rides in an elevator."

"Anyone?" said Leo.

"Anyone who follows the three rules of the game," replied Sam. He had read about them on the Internet.

"Rule number one, you have to use the elevator after people go home from work," he said. "Rule number two, you have to pick a building that has at least fourteen floors. And then —"

"Why fourteen?" asked Leo.

"Because the fourteenth floor is actually the thirteenth," said Sam. "Lots of buildings don't count the thirteenth floor because the number thirteen is bad luck. Instead, the floor numbers go from twelve to fourteen."

"Have you done it?" asked Leo.

Sam stared at his friend. Then he looked out the bus window and stared at the tall office buildings that lined the street. Some of the windows were still brightly lit, but others were already dark. "Not yet," said Sam. "But I know some kids who did it. Do you remember Raymond Garcia from Mr. Barker's class? His family had to move away because Raymond saw the ghost. His hair turned white, and he couldn't speak. Now he's in a hospital all the time."

Leo looked at Sam, but the other boy wouldn't look him in the eye. *Just a story*, thought Leo. If that Raymond kid couldn't talk, how did they know what happened to him?

"So which building did Raymond go to?" asked Leo.

"The Graver," said Sam.

The bus wheezed to a stop at a busy street corner. More passengers got on.

"Hey, this is 8th Street," said Leo. "I gotta go." Leo grabbed his backpack, jumped up from the seat, and swung out the side door.

"Wait!" said Sam. "I didn't tell you about rule number three —"

Leo was already outside when Sam finished talking. He waved at Sam's pale face in the window. Sam's eyes were big and he was mouthing some words. *Don't look at . . .*

"What?" Leo asked. He cupped his hand to his ear.

The bus roared and pulled away. *What did Sam say?* Leo asked himself. *Don't look at her? Don't look at* who?

On the sidewalk, a flood of gloomy workers surrounded Leo. He had never seen so many. The murmuring crowd shoved him first one way, then another. He almost lost hold of his backpack. He was turned around so many times that he finally he lost his sense of direction. He couldn't even see a street sign.

Leo forced his way out of the mob. He leaned against the side of a building to catch his breath. Something bony pressed against his back. He turned and saw metal letters jutting out from the wall. GRAVER BUILDING.

Sam felt his skin prickling. This was the building. He walked over to the glass doors and gazed in. The lobby looked deserted. Only a few lights were still on. There was a guard sitting at a desk, but he was sleeping.

Leo hadn't planned on trying that stupid game, but something was pulling him into the building. It was almost as if he couldn't help himself.

It was just a game, after all. Leo wanted to prove to Sam and everyone else that the story about Raymond was fake.

There is no such thing as ghosts, Leo told himself. *Especially here. Ghosts haunt old houses, not office buildings.*

Leo stepped into the lobby. He saw two old-fashioned elevator doors near the back.

He quietly walked toward the elevators and pushed the up button. Above each door was a row of lights, indicating which floor the elevator was on and if it was moving. The one on the right was stuck on the fourteenth floor. The one on the left was moving quickly toward the lobby. Eighth floor, seventh floor, sixth floor —

When the elevator on the left reached the lobby, the door slid open. No one was inside.

Leo hesitated for just a moment. Then he rushed inside before he could change his mind. He pushed the button for the fourteenth floor, and the door slid shut with a hiss.

Smoothly, the elevator rose, dinging as it passed floor after floor. When it reached the fourteenth floor — really the thirteenth — the door opened. No one was waiting for it. *All the workers must be gone,* Leo thought. He stepped out of the elevator for a quick look around. The sound of a vacuum cleaner came from the end of the hall. *Must be a maintenance worker cleaning up for the night.*

Hiss! The elevator door slid shut.

Leo turned around. He reached for the down button that was on the wall between the two doors, but then he noticed something. The elevator on the right, the one that had been sitting on the fourteenth floor all along, was still there. The door was open.

Leo stepped inside. He pushed the button for the lobby and waited. The door closed without a sound.

Well, that's that, thought Leo. *Now I can tell Sam his story was a fake. Just one of those dumb urban legends that everyone talks about.*

The elevator stopped on the seventh floor. The door opened onto a dark, silent hallway. No one was there.

Leo punched the lobby button again. *Hiss,* and the elevator descended once more. He watched the lights above the inside of the door. Sixth floor, fifth floor, fourth floor . . .

The hum of the moving elevator grew to a loud groan, and then suddenly went silent. All the lights went out. Leo felt the elevator grind to a stop.

Leo could see nothing. He heard a soft noise from somewhere behind him. Someone was breathing. *Or is that my heart beating?* Leo wondered. He reached blindly toward the buttons. When his hands reached them, the plastic buttons were icy cold. He slapped at them wildly, hitting as many as he could.

Zhooom!

Suddenly, the elevator jerked and started moving again. The lights snapped on.

Leo whipped around to see where the breathing sound was coming from. He was alone. Leo thought, *I'm just letting Sam's story get to me.* He swallowed hard and adjusted the backpack on his shoulders. He would be glad to get out of there. The elevator came to a smooth stop and the door slid open.

"What!" yelled Leo. He wasn't at the lobby. Instead he found himself in a dark gray hallway. It looked like a basement.

"Stupid elevator," he said impatiently. "I'm never getting out of here."

"Oh yes, you will," a voice whispered from behind him.

A tall woman stood in the corner. Long black hair covered her face. Her clothes were torn and burned.

She reached a thin white hand toward Leo. He cried out and bumped up against the wall. The white hand moved past him to press the button for the lobby. Leo watched, frozen, as the door closed quickly.

"Don't worry," the woman whispered. "You won't be here long." Her straight black hair seemed to move like curtains in a night wind. "What's the worst that could happen?" she asked.

Then the lights went out.

ERASED

Thunder boomed outside the classroom, and Mrs. Denton raised her voice to be heard. "Quiet, class. We've all heard thunder before. Everyone get out your drawing pencils."

Holli opened the lid of her desk. She was about to grab the colored pencils she always used for art class, but a metallic gleam caught her eye.

I forgot all about this, thought Holli, reaching in and pushing aside some papers.

For her birthday two months ago, Aunt Olive had given her a pencil box with an orange dragon on the lid. The dragon was blowing fire. Holli picked it up and followed the swirls of gold and yellow flame onto the back of the box. When she turned the box back around, the dragon was gone. Instead, swooshes of orange fire decorated the front. *Weird,* thought Holli. *Maybe I just thought all those swooshes looked like a dragon.*

Holli popped opened the lid. The smell of burnt caramel swirled into her nose. Inside were twelve colored pencils and a bright red eraser printed with the words "Magical Eraser." The words seemed to wiggle, like waves of heat off of pavement in the summertime.

Another rumble of thunder shook the room as Mrs. Denton opened her mouth to speak again. "Before you begin drawing," she said, "describe what you see. Write down a sentence and tell us what you are looking at."

The boy sitting in front of Holli raised his hand. "What do we look at?" he asked.

"Good question, Russell," answered Mrs. Denton. "Look at anything at all. It could be something from your desk, something in the room. Or even outside the windows."

Holli looked outside. There was not much to see. Dark clouds had filled the sky. Lightning flashed and thunder rumbled. Tree branches bent in the wind.

She started writing with the new brown pencil: *The girl watched the lightning through the window and listened to the thunder.*

Holli rubbed her nose and frowned. *Boring,* she thought. Mrs. Denton was always teaching them to use "vivid language." How did the lightning flash? How did the thunder sound? How did the girl feel as she watched the storm?

She grabbed the eraser from the pencil box.

"Ow!" she exclaimed. She dropped the eraser onto her desk. A few students turned to look at her. The eraser had felt hot, like the buckles on her backpack when she left it lying in the sun. Holli stared at the bright red block of rubber. She carefully touched it with the tip of her finger. But now it was cool.

Holli picked up the eraser and looked at the sentence. She decided to start over, and began erasing the sentence from the end. First the period, then the word "thunder."

A few rows away, a student gasped. "The thunder stopped!" she whispered. Several students around her mumbled and raised their heads to listen.

Holli didn't notice them. She was busy erasing her sentence: *The girl watched the lightning through the window and listened to the*

She rubbed out the next four words. When she erased the word "window," a girl cried out, "Mrs. Denton! Where's the window?"

Holli looked up. The constant thunder had stopped rumbling. The window on the side of the room was gone. Instead of glass there was a brick wall painted beige, like the other three walls of the classroom. Mrs. Denton stood at the front of the room, her mouth hanging open, staring at the new wall.

A flash of lightning startled the class. A cold fear prickled Holli's scalp. How could there still be lightning without a window to see it through?

More and more students started shouting.

"Where's the window?"

"What's happening?"

"I want to go home!"

Holli looked down at her shortening sentence, then at the eraser in her hand. *That's impossible,* she told herself. *It's just an eraser.* Carefully she rubbed out the next two words — "through the" — but nothing happened.

She started on the next word, and as soon as she had erased the letters *ning*, the lightning stopped. The students' cries and shouts grew quieter. The panic seemed to melt away.

Mrs. Denton looked more relaxed. "All right, class," she said. "Let's settle down. I'll call the custodian about the window —"

Without thinking, Holli continued erasing the sentence. The word "light" disappeared, and suddenly the classroom was wrapped in darkness.

Screams and shouts surrounded Holli. She heard the scraping of chairs and desks as students jumped up in fear and began to run. She couldn't see anything. But she still had her pencil and eraser. If she wrote the word "light" again, would everything go back to normal?

Someone bumped into her desk. Startled, Holli dropped both her pencil and her eraser. She heard the metal pencil box clatter on the vinyl floor. The screams grew louder. Mrs. Denton was weeping somewhere in the dark.

Holli dropped to her knees and quickly felt around on the floor. If she could just find that pencil. Legs and shoes brushed past her. No light could enter the room without the window, and with all the students running and stumbling it made it harder to find the way out.

All those feet running and shuffling and tripping past her. What if someone stepped on the eraser? What if that red block of rubber got trapped beneath a shoe? A shoe that was moving, running, rubbing the eraser against the floor? Rubbing and rubbing . . .

Oh, no, thought Holli. *Not the floor!*

Suddenly, everything in the room — desks, chairs, books, pencils, and backpacks — and everyone began falling . . .

Falling . . .

Falling forever into unending darkness . . . a darkness without a floor . . .

I ONLY SEE
CHOCOLATE

"I love, love, love chocolate!" exclaimed Sara.

She and her friends Holly and Aruna were standing outside the new bakery. Bright June sunshine shone on the front window and freshly painted golden letters read:

ORBWICH SISTERS BAKED GOODS & SWEETS

A sign on the door announced:

Opening Day!

"Look at that éclair!" Aruna pointed.

"That can't be an éclair," said Holly. "It's too big."

"I know," replied Aruna, smiling. "Yum!"

Sara had her eye on a double-decker cake stand covered with dozens of small, dark globes. "Chocolate-covered cherries," read the sign. *My absolute favorite*, thought Sara.

"Who's going in first?" asked Holly. "I want to see Aruna eat that monster éclair!"

The bakery had been an empty storefront just the day before. Now it stood like a shiny gingerbread house, with candy-colored decorations and a bright yellow door. Sara pushed it open, making a bell jingle sweetly as she and her friends stepped inside.

A dozen customers were already there, browsing through shelves and tables and cases. The tiny store was filled with breads, cakes and cupcakes, cookies, donuts, and — Sara spied them at once — chocolate-covered cherries.

"Red velvet cupcakes!" said Holly.

"This place smells like my grandma's cookie jar!" said Aruna.

Sara left her friends staring at goodies while she walked toward the big glass cases at the back of the store. Two women stood behind the cases and handed customers their chosen sweets from the loaded shelves.

A third woman stood at the cash register ringing up bags full of baked goods. They each wore a gleaming white apron, a soft white chef's cap, and a pair of dark sunglasses.

That's rude, thought Sara. Sara's mother had taught her it was impolite to wear sunglasses indoors.

One of the women behind the case turned toward Sara. "Can I help you, young lady?" she asked.

Next to the woman's mouth was a large mole with three hairs growing out of it. Sara tried hard not to stare at it.

"There are other customers waiting behind you," said the woman gently.

"Oh, sorry," said Sara. "I'll have five chocolate-covered cherries."

"Excellent choice," said the woman. "My favorite."

"Mine too!" echoed Sara.

The woman dropped five of the chocolate globes into a crisp white bag. "I'll tell you a secret," she whispered, handing the bag over the counter. "These taste better when they're eaten fresh."

The girl felt the warmth of the chocolate through the crisp paper. She smelled the thick, sweet scent, and her mouth watered.

"Sara!" Aruna bumped into her with a giggle. "Guess what? I got *two* éclairs! And I don't care how big they are."

Holly joined them. She was holding a bag bigger than either of theirs. "Cupcakes," she explained. "For my family."

The woman at the register took Sara's money and handed back her change. She smiled widely. Her teeth looked like little sugar cubes.

The bell over the door jingled again as the girls stepped outside. They walked together quietly for several minutes, each girl absorbed in eating her own special treat.

Sara had chewed three of the delicious chocolate-covered cherries when she asked, "Where do you think they came from?"

"The cherries?" asked Aruna.

"No, I mean those ladies. They looked sort of weird to me," said Sara.

"And what's with the sunglasses?" said Holly.

"I know!" said Sara.

"Who cares?" asked Aruna. "Their treats are delicious." She stuffed the rest of a dripping éclair into her already-full mouth.

Holly and Sara nodded in agreement.

A few quiet minutes passed. Sara had another chocolate-covered cherry. "But I mean, like, the bakery wasn't even there yesterday," Sara said. "No signs or anything."

"My mother said there was nothing in the newspaper, either," said Holly. Her family lived across the street from the new bakery. Her mother had seen the store just that morning and told Holly about it. And Holly had called her friends.

"And how would they have time to bake everything?" asked Sara.

"They'd need tons of butter and sugar and chocolate and stuff," added Holly. "But there were no cars or trucks around."

Aruna giggled. "Maybe they're witches," she said. Then she whispered, "Did you see the hairy mole on that one behind the counter?"

"So they just waved a wand and made everything magically appear?" said Holly.

The hot June sun warmed the girls' hands and faces. Sara reached for another cherry. The chocolates had started melting in the bag, and when she pulled out the next one, some of the chocolate had dripped away, revealing the bright red cherry underneath.

Sara looked closer. It wasn't a cherry.

It was an eye.

A human eye.

THE
LOOSE
NAIL

Austin O'Connor looked up from his comic book and stared out the car window. They had been driving for hours, but all he had seen was hills and grass. More hills and more grass. This time he noticed a few trees. Then, his father turned onto a dirt road, and Austin immediately unbuckled his seat belt.

Mrs. O'Connor glanced over her shoulder from the front seat.

"Keep your seat belt on," she told Austin. "I know we're not on the main highway anymore, but driving is still dangerous."

Austin thought his mother worried too much.

"And remember," said Mr. O'Connor, not taking his eyes off the road, "Grandma gets very lonely way out here."

"She hasn't seen you since you were a baby," added his mother, smiling.

During the long drive, Austin had realized he couldn't remember actually seeing his grandmother. Only pictures of her. She didn't have a computer and only used an old-fashioned landline phone. In fact, he wondered why they were visiting her now, after all this time. His parents didn't say anything about a birthday. Was there a special reason for driving all the way out into the country?

"Yes, she's quite lonely," his father said. "And sometimes lonely people do, uh, different things."

"What do you mean, different things?" asked Austin.

"Oh George, really!" said Mrs. O'Connor.

"It's true," said Mr. O'Connor. Then he glanced at Austin in the rearview mirror. "Your Grandma has . . . hobbies to pass the time."

"Everyone has hobbies," said Mrs. O'Connor.

"All I'm saying is, if Grandma seems a little different," continued Austin's father, "just remember that she doesn't get a chance to see people a lot. Real people, that is."

The car made another turn in the winding road. Austin saw an enormous old farmhouse surrounded by birch trees and a wide green lawn. His father pulled the car to a stop in front of the house.

Austin and his parents climbed out of their car. His mother leaned in and grabbed a large tote bag that had been sitting on the floor by her feet. It looked heavy. "I can carry that," said Austin.

"No!" his mother said sharply, pulling the bag to her chest. She put on a quick smile. "It's fine, dear. I can manage myself, but thanks for offering."

An old woman greeted them from the porch. Austin waved back. "Hi, Grandma," he said. He walked up the front wooden steps and found himself in a soft, warm embrace.

"Oh my, you've grown so much," said the old woman, her tiny wrinkled face close to Austin's.

"How are you, Mom?" asked Mrs. O'Connor.

"You've done such a good job raising your boy," she replied. "I can tell. Just look at him."

Austin was looking at the wide lawn. He couldn't see the main road, hidden a mile away behind walls of trees.

"Sure is quiet here," said Austin.

"And so much to do," said Grandma. "My family keeps me so busy. And my knitting, of course."

"Family?" asked Austin. "But I thought you lived all alone out here."

Austin's mother gave him a shushing look, but it was too late. Grandma was opening the front door and waving Austin inside.

"Before we have lunch on the porch," she said, "you must come in and say hello."

Austin's eyes took a moment to adjust from the bright sunshine outside. He stood in a large dim room that was crammed with a forest of furniture — chairs, tables, cabinets, ottomans, and sofas. At first, Austin thought everything was covered with blankets and pillows. Then he realized they were people. People knitted from yarn.

Some yarn people sat on the chairs with smaller yarn figures on their laps. A family of dolls was squeezed together on a sofa. Other dolls sat at the tables, with cups of coffee in front of them. A couple of yarn kittens perched on windowsills.

"Did . . . did you make all these?" Austin asked.

Grandma smiled. "Of course, dear. That's Grandma's job."

Austin crept over to a boy-shaped yarn figure sitting on a low stool. The figure was the same size as he was. Realistic-looking yarn ears were sewn to each side of the head. Austin put out a hand to touch it.

"I see you're making a friend," said Grandma.

Austin pulled his hand away. The yarn ear had twitched! Slowly, the yarn boy's head turned. One of its arms reached toward Austin. Austin yelled and backed away. Then he noticed that several of the bigger yarn figures were also turning to look at him. A doll at one of the tables knocked over a coffee cup. He thought he heard a gasp from one of the knitted mouths.

"Well, aren't you going to say hello to your cousins?" said Grandma. "After all, this is a family reunion."

Austin screamed and ran out the front door. He raced across the porch and down the wooden stairs. He did not see the loose nail sticking up from one of the steps.

"Austin!" his mother shouted.

Faster and faster the boy ran. He had to get away. Something wasn't right. How could the dolls move like that? And what did Grandma mean when she said they were his cousins?

Austin kept running. He wouldn't stop until he reached the main road. Suddenly, he fell to the ground. He looked down and saw, below his shorts, his left leg was missing. In its place was a long flesh-colored strand of yarn, winding all the way back to the front porch and to the loose nail that had caught against Austin's foot.

"Austin!" He heard the old woman's voice. She was walking across the grass, winding up the string of yarn into a ball as she went.

"Dear, dear," she said. "You'll have to stay with me for a while. I can't have you go home looking like that."

The old woman looked off into the clouds, her thoughts far away. "I remember when I first made you for your mother. The poor dear couldn't have children, so I helped out. I love knitting. And you made her so happy."

Then she turned to glance back at her distant house. "It's a good thing your mother brought all that extra yarn with her," she said. "You need to grow a little more before school starts again. We want you just as tall as the other boys."

THE
MONSTER
IN THE
MAILBOX

Mr. Howard Finn, the neighborhood's new mailman, had never met anyone like Dory before. The little girl never stopped talking.

"This one's Mrs. Gomez's house. She has twelve grandchildren. Twelve's a lot, isn't it? She must get a lot of presents for her birthday. I like presents. Especially games and puzzles. But I don't want grandchildren. I wonder what kind of presents Mrs. Gomez gets."

Dory was eight years old with pumpkin-colored hair. Mr. Finn had met her as soon as he stepped out of his mail truck. He was hauling the heavy mailbag over his shoulder when Dory appeared at his side. She told him she would help him because this was his first day.

"It's not my first day delivering the mail," Mr. Finn had pointed out. "But it is my first day in your neighborhood."

"My family just moved in a few weeks ago, so I know what it feels like," Dory said.

Mr. Finn had dropped off mail, and a few packages, to four of the neighborhood homes when he asked about Dory's house. The little girl frowned and pointed across the street.

"That's a big house," said Mr. Finn. Four stories of glass and steel towered above the nearby houses. No trees or bushes or flowers grew in the yard. Instead, there were a dozen boulders — big boulders — scattered across a field of white gravel. Mr. Finn thought it looked more like a machine than a house. No wonder the little girl was frowning.

Mr. Finn kept talking while he dug into his bag for the next customer's mail. He didn't want to let go of his end of the conversation, or Dory might start chattering again.

"Do you have any brothers or sisters?" he asked.

Dory shook her head. "Not really," she said.

Mr. Finn thought that was an odd answer.

Dory added, "But I have a pet —"

"Oh, that's nice," the man said. "I always liked pets when I was a boy. Dog or cat?"

Dory shook her head again.

"A hamster, maybe?" asked Mr. Finn.

"It's a monster," said Dory, smiling.

"Oh, I see," said Mr. Finn. This little girl really was odd. "A monster, huh? Is he a nice monster?"

"It's a girl monster," said Dory. "She's very nice. But sometimes she gets very, very hungry."

Mr. Finn walked across Mrs. Gomez's yard and up the front steps of her house. He slipped the mail through a slot in the door, and then started toward the next house, the Hendersons'. The last one on that block. "So do you let your monster play in the yard?" asked Mr. Finn.

"She's not allowed outside," said Dory. "That makes her very sad."

"So where do you keep her?" the man asked while digging into his mailbag again.

"She's in the mailbox."

Mr. Finn stopped digging and looked down at the girl. Dory was busy pulling clovers from the Hendersons' lawn. "Ten, eleven, twelve," she counted. The man glanced across the street at her house, the glass-and-steel giant. After this block, Dory's house was next on his route.

Then he saw the mailbox. It looked ordinary, a small metal box sitting atop a post. It stood at the bottom of concrete steps that led up to Dory's front yard with the boulders and the white gravel.

"She lives in the mailbox?" repeated Mr. Finn. "She must be a little monster, then."

"Nuh-uh," said Dory. "She's big."

Mr. Finn walked slowly across the Hendersons' yard to the next-door house, never taking his eyes off of the mailbox across the street. "If she's so big, how does she fit in there?" he asked quietly.

Dory giggled. "She's all squishy and squashy," said the little girl. "I just push her really hard and she pops right in."

Mr. Finn had decided that Dory was clearly strange. But she also had a big imagination. *Typical lonely, bright child,* he thought. Like he had been as a boy. *Probably doesn't have any friends in the neighborhood yet,* he told himself. *Which is why she's following me.*

He dropped the mail at the last house on the block and then slowly started across the street.

"Yay!" said Dory. Then she sang, "We're going to my house!"

Mr. Finn looked at her mailbox again. Squishy, squashy. And didn't the kid say her pet was very, very hungry? Or was he just making that up?

The man reached into his bag and pulled out the few envelopes that were addressed to Dory's house. He held them out to the little girl. "Here," he said, trying to smile. "You can give them to your parents."

"Oh, no," said Dory. "I'm not supposed to touch the mail. Daddy says it's too important. It has to go in the mailbox."

Mr. Finn licked his lips. "But it's only a few —"

"No!" said Dory. She stamped her foot. "It has to go in the mailbox."

Mr. Finn straightened his back. He held his head up. *I'm a grown man,* he told himself. *This is ridiculous, to be frightened by some little girl's story.* He stepped closer to the mailbox. Dory stepped aside to give him more room. Her eyes grew wide. She even stopped talking.

The mailman reached out with both hands.

One held the letters, the other gripped the metal tab on top of the mailbox door.

He took a deep breath.

"Nooooo!" wailed Dory. "She's gone!"

Mr. Finn opened his eyes. He hadn't even realized he had closed them. He didn't remember opening the mailbox. But the door was open and the inside was as normal as every other one he'd seen. An ordinary metal box. That's all it was.

"Where did she go?" cried Dory.

Mr. Finn felt sorry for the girl. "Maybe she was feeling too squished in there," he said. "Maybe she's looking for another mailbox."

"But she liked *this* mailbox!" said Dory.

Mr. Finn walked back to his truck. Over his shoulder, he waved to Dory and called out, "See you tomorrow."

Dory was frowning but she still waved. "Tomorrow," she mumbled. Then she turned and started trudging up the concrete steps to her front yard.

The little girl heard a scream. It came from the mail truck. The truck was rocking back and forth. She could see through the windows on the side that seven long, black tentacles, covered in blood-red suckers, were twisting and thrashing inside. She spotted Mr. Finn's white face pressed up against the glass, then he was gone.

Dory sighed happily. Maybe the nice mailman was right. Maybe her pet was getting a little too big for the mailbox.

PLEASE DON'T TOUCH THE BUS DRIVER

Grace kept hoping that her grandmother wouldn't say anything embarrassing during their trip to the museum.

Too late.

They hadn't even reached the museum when it happened. In fact, they were standing at the bus stop only two blocks from Grandmother's house when the old woman looked around at the commuters and snorted. Grace's grandmother always made that sound right before she said something terrible.

"People don't look you in the face anymore," said her grandmother. Grace thought her voice was much too loud. "Everyone's gawking at their little screen-things."

Screen things. She means phones or tablets, Grace thought.

"People used to talk to each other," her grandmother continued. "You used to stand here on the sidewalk and have an actual conversation with your neighbors. Using words. Out loud. Not anymore. Not when they've got their faces buried in those little Google-machines."

Grace's grandmother had once caught her working on her laptop at home. That's when the older woman first heard of Google. Now every device was a Google-machine. Grace squirmed, hoping that no one else at the bus stop was listening.

Then another snort.

"Even if you did want to talk," said her grandmother, "people can't hear you because they all wear those little ear plugs."

"They're called earbuds, Grandma," said Grace.

"Huh?" said the old woman.

"They're earbuds," Grace said patiently.

"Ear pumps?"

"*Buds*, like buds on a tree," said Grace. "That's what they sort of look like."

"A stupid name for a stupid thing," said her grandmother. "Please tell me you'll never wear that kind of contraption, Grace."

Grace didn't know how to answer. She had earbuds in her backpack right now, in fact, coiled up next to her iPad. Luckily, a bus came into view at that moment.

"The bus," she said. Grace couldn't wait until they arrived at the museum. Maybe if her grandmother were surrounded by old stuff, like paintings and statues, she wouldn't feel so cranky.

"People don't hear a thing you say anymore." Her grandmother didn't show any signs of calming down. "It's rude, that's what it is. Downright rude!"

The bus halted and the door opened with a hiss.

"Rude!" the old woman repeated.

The bus driver was a young man with long black hair and big ears. As passengers climbed onto the bus, he just stared out the big front window and swayed his head back and forth. He was wearing earbuds. Grace felt sick to her stomach.

Please, please, please don't say anything, the girl kept repeating in her mind.

Grandmother climbed to the top of the steps. She gave one look at the young bus driver and snorted. "Young man," she said.

"What's wrong, Grandma?" asked Grace, quickly stepping up next to her.

"How does he know where to stop if he can't hear me?" she exclaimed. She turned to the driver again. "Young man!"

Grace glanced at the other passengers. They were all staring at her grandmother and two or three were staring to mumble. The bus driver closed the door, revved the engine, and pulled away from the curb. Grandmother held on to a metal pole, but would not sit down.

"Young man, can you hear me?" she said. She put her face inches from his head.

The bus driver ignored her. *His music must be really loud*, thought Grace.

"This is ridiculous!" said her grandmother. She reached out and grasped the cord of the earbuds that lay resting on the driver's chest. She pulled, and the buds popped out of both ears. With a triumphant smile, the old woman began, "Now, will you listen —"

Her voice was drowned out by a loud hissing sound. It was not the bus door. It reminded Grace of air escaping from a balloon.

Grandmother screamed and fell back into an empty seat.

The hiss was coming from the ears of the young driver. Grace stared, speechless, as the man collapsed into himself. His head sank onto his neck, his chest caved in, and his hands shrank and dropped off of the steering wheel. His legs shriveled up and hung from the seat like deflated balloons.

The driver's seat was quickly covered with a blob of empty skin.

"Help! Do something!" the old woman yelled. Only Grace heard her. All the other passengers were busy listening to their earbuds or staring at their little screens.

ROLLER
GHOSTER

Ricky and Oscar couldn't remember how many times they'd ridden the roller coaster that weekend.

"Best. Ride. Ever!" said Ricky.

"That was awesome!" said Oscar.

The Killer Comet roller coaster inside the Richdale shopping mall was one of the fastest in the world. The twisting, plunging track was less than a mile long, but at one dramatic drop, nicknamed the Dark Star, it reached a speed of 150 miles per hour. The speed was what drew such long lines to the ride. The speed was also responsible for the ride's one deadly accident.

"Have you heard about the ghost on this ride?" said a boy to his girlfriend. They were standing in line ahead of Ricky and Oscar. The girl shook her head. "A kid died," he said. "He jumped off or was thrown off at the Dark Star drop. And some people say they see him still riding it."

The girl gasped.

Oscar rolled his eyes. He and Ricky had been hearing this story for years. It didn't stop them from riding the Killer Comet whenever they had a chance.

In less than ten minutes, they were boarding the roller coaster. The couple sat just in front of them in the same car. The outside of each car was built to look like a small rocket. A blazing golden number was painted on the front.

"Uh oh, Annie," said the boy in front of them. "We got Car Thirteen."

"Stop it, Ryan," said Annie. "I'm only going on this once, and that's it. Don't make it even harder for me."

"But thirteen is an unlucky number . . ." Ryan continued.

"I said stop, Ryan, or I'm getting off!"

"Too late," he said.

The safety bars came down, locking everyone into their seats. Ricky and Oscar were so used to the ride that they never even held on to the bar anymore. In front of them, Annie gripped the bar with white knuckles.

"And we're off!" shouted Oscar.

A powerful cable under the track pulled the train of cars up, up, up toward the first and tallest peak.

"I can't look!" wailed Annie.

The train slowly crested the peak, and then swiftly, almost without warning, it plunged down the steep slope, accompanied by passengers' screams and cries and laughter. Up and down and around again the train rocketed along the track.

"What's that?" screamed Annie, pointing ahead of them.

The roller coaster track seemed almost vertical as it plunged inside a fake mountainside covered with trolls and ogres.

"That's the Dark Star," said Ryan. "Hold on!"

"Ooh!" said Oscar, holding his arms up over his head. "Watch out for the ghoooooost!"

The air seemed to rush out of their bodies as the train shot inside the mountain. Blackness swallowed up the cars. There was silence during this part of the ride. Passengers were too scared to scream.

Then, finally, the slope became more gradual and the train began to slow.

"Smile!" shouted Ryan.

In a few moments, the ride was over. Passengers were laughing and shouting and jumping out of the cars.

"Let's stop over by the photo booth," said Ricky, grinning, to his friend.

They followed close behind Ryan and Annie as the couple made their way to the booth near the foot of the roller coaster.

There was a camera that snapped pictures of each car as it plunged into the Dark Star. For a few dollars, people could buy the photos.

Ryan and Annie looked at their photo as it came up on the big display screen.

"Ha! There we are," said Ryan.

"I look like a scared cat," Annie said, laughing.

Ryan gripped Annie's arm. "Wait," he said. "Those two kids behind us."

"What two kids?" said Annie.

Ryan pointed. "See those two boys sitting in the seat behind us?"

"That seat was empty," said Annie.

"That seat's always empty," said the redheaded man running the photo booth. "That's Car Thirteen. That's the car the two kids fell out of twenty years ago."

The photo of Ryan and Annie showed the outlines of two boys sitting directly behind them. Their faces could barely be seen, but it looked as if they were laughing.

"I want to go home," said Annie.

Oscar and Ricky chuckled as they watched the couple hurry out of the park.

"Want to go again?" asked Oscar.

"I'm dying to," said Ricky with a smile.

MOTHER
WHO

There are just too many, thought Mia. *Way too many!*

"You have to choose one, Mia," said her mother. "Only one."

Mia was staring at the cereal boxes stacked on the shelves in front of her. There had to be twenty or thirty different brands. Each one was packaged in a colorful box with a cute name and an even cuter cartoon character.

"Hurry up, Mia," said her mother. "I have a lot more items on my list." The woman tightened her grip on the shopping cart, wheeled down the aisle, and then disappeared around the corner. "Just one!" her mother called out.

I give up, Mia thought. How could she choose between *Kiddy Bits* or *Chock o' Chocolate* or *Pretty Pony Puffs*?

Mia's family wasn't poor, but her mom was always careful with money. When they went to the store, it was always the same: one brand of cereal, one brand of juice, one brand of cheese. Mia decided she needed more flavors in her life. Which is exactly what it said on the *Kiddy Bits* box: "Taste every flavor in every bite!"

So Mia stopped thinking and started grabbing. *We can afford it,* she decided.

She ended up with five different brands — the most she could carry at one time. Then she headed down the aisle and saw her mother wheel into sight with her cart.

"There you are, Mia," her mother exclaimed. "What took you so long?"

Mia was about to answer when she heard a familiar voice behind her. "Mia!"

She turned and saw her mother with the shopping cart at the other end of the aisle.

"Hurry up!" said the second mother. "We have to run to the pharmacy after this."

"Mia, what are you standing there for?" asked the first mother.

Bang! Another shopper's cart bumped into her mother's — the first mother's — cart. "Sorry!" said the shopper. When the shopper came into view, Mia saw that it was another woman who looked exactly like her mother. In fact, all three women looked exactly like each other, but they wore different clothes.

One wore jeans and black sandals, another wore a flowery skirt and scarf, and the third was in dressy slacks and a sweater with a colorful headband. Their carts were full of different items. But none of them seemed to notice that they were exact copies of one another.

Mia was too startled to speak or move. Who was her real mother? She couldn't remember what her mother was wearing when they had arrived at the store.

Mia cried out, "Mom!"

"Yes, honey?" the trio called together.

Too many, thought Mia. *How do I choose?*

The girl dropped her cereal boxes and ran toward the end of the aisle, the end where only one of her mothers stood, the one wearing the flowery skirt. As she ran past the cart, the woman called out, "Mia! Where do you think you're going?" She reached out to Mia, but the girl was too quick.

A voice rang out over the store loudspeaker. "Clean up in aisle six. Cereal boxes down."

A moment later, Mia stood outside in the grocery store's parking lot, stopping to catch her breath. Her hands were shaking. She wanted to go home. She wanted her mother. But *which* mother?

Tears began to flood Mia's eyes. *How did this happen?* Mia wondered. She had just been standing in the aisle, trying to decide which cereal to choose when — that was it! She had wanted more than one box of cereal. Did some part of her also want more than one mother? Had she caused her mother to turn into three different versions?

If I think hard enough, maybe the clones will disappear and only my real mom will remain, Mia thought. *With her one brand of milk, one brand of soft drink, one day a week to do any type of shopping, and always at the same boring stores . . .*

But maybe there was another choice. One of the other two mothers might be more fun. Someone who laughed and shopped and loved spending money on her wonderful daughter. A happy mother, who was more easy-going.

Mia thought hard. She tried picturing the kind of mother she really wanted.

Concentrating was hard work. Mia dashed away from the doors and into the parking lot to find their car. She would wait there for her mother, one mother, to come and drive them both home. On her way to the parking lot, Mia wondered if she'd find three blue SUVs in a row, all with the same license plate.

But the car stood alone. Her mom's blue SUV was where they'd parked it. Mia knew the doors would be locked. But the sun was shining and the air was warm, so she decided to stand around and wait.

Mia kept her eye on the grocery store's front doors.

There! Her mother was leaving the store, pushing the cart. And there was only one!

Yes! she thought. *Finally.*

Mia leaned back against the car and smiled. She closed her eyes, letting the sun warm her face.

"Mia," came her mother's voice. "Why did you grab five cereal boxes?"

Mia opened her eyes. The SUV was surrounded by fourteen or fifteen women who all looked alike. Each one stood behind a shopping cart filled with grocery bags. Each one stared at Mia.

"I told you to pick just one," said all the mothers at once. "Now you've gone and made it harder."

The circle of women tightened around Mia and the car. They stepped closer and closer.

"Pick one, Mia!" they chanted. "Pick one! Pick one! Pick ONE!

SOMETHING'S WRONG WITH LOCKER 307

Dear Principal Pirelli,

My name is Jeremy Hawke. I am a student here at Lovecraft Middle School, and I have to warn you about something really bad. There's something wrong with locker 307. My locker is number 306. It is perfectly okay except for the dried gum on the inside door that I can't get rid of. And the hinges squeak. But locker 307 is dangerous. Really and truly dangerous. I know that sounds crazy. I would come tell you in person, but I thought it would be better to write all this down in case I forgot anything important.

Don't let any kid use that locker. Please!!!!

You probably have a computer report somewhere about all the lockers and all the kids who used them over the years. Well, look up whoever was assigned locker 307. It's in the newer section of school. Do you notice anything weird?

This fall, the kid who had that locker next to mine, 307, was Haruki Mizo. We call him Rookie. I mean, we used to, when he was still here.

The second week of school I noticed that he carried all of his books around all the time. One day in the library, we were working on a geography project together. I asked him, "Why don't you leave some of your books in your locker?" He shook his head and didn't say anything.

Then I said, "Is it broken? Sometimes the lockers get broken and the custodians don't even know it."

"It opens," said Haruki. His voice sounded funny, like he was far away.

Then he got up from the table and walked out of the library. We were supposed to be partners, but he just walked away. Didn't say another word. I thought maybe he was sick. He looked sort of pale.

We didn't talk about the locker again until about a week ago. School was over, and I had stayed late for the Science Fiction and Manga Club meeting. I was at my locker, getting my geography book for homework and slipping it into my backpack, when I heard something inside Haruki's locker. It sounded like a baby crying. I walked closer to his locker and put my ear up by the vents. The noise was clearer and louder. It didn't sound like a baby anymore, but like an animal howling in the distance.

I looked around to see if anyone else nearby could hear it. The halls were empty. Then I spied Haruki standing at the end of the row of lockers.

"What's in there?" I asked.

A bang from the locker startled me. A deep growl came through the locker vents. Then another bang. Something on the other side of the door was trying to get out.

I dropped my backpack and ran over to Haruki. "We have to tell someone," I said. "We have to tell the principal."

"No," he said. "No, I can't." At first, I thought he was going to cry. Then he said, "I'm sorry."

"What are you talking about?" I said.

"I'm sorry you know about the locker," he said. Then his eyes got all cold and creepy, like he was a robot or something. He stared and stared. "You heard it, didn't you?" he said. "It's too late now. You heard it."

The locker door rattled.

Haruki looked at the locker. "It won't get out," he said quietly. "It doesn't need to."

"What is going on?" I was practically shouting at him.

"You know the kid who had that locker before me?" he asked.

I didn't.

"Her name was Alice Johnson," he said.

"You mean Weird Alice?" I said. "I remember her. She moved last year, right before summer vacation."

"She didn't move," Haruki said. "She disappeared. So did her family."

Haruki was creeping me out. "How do you know that?"

"I heard the story from one of Alice's friends after she disappeared," said Haruki. "When I was assigned Alice's locker, number 307, Denise Gonzales told me that Alice was afraid of it."

My stomach turned to ice. Denise Gonzales was a girl who had been in our grade. She had left school earlier this year. No one heard why she left. There were all kinds of rumors — that her parents were spies, that they were wanted by the police. The one thing we knew for certain was that she was gone, and so was her family.

"Anyone who has that locker," said Haruki, "or hears about what it does . . . they . . . they . . ."

"They what?" I shouted.

"They disappear," said Haruki.

This was getting stupid. Now I was mad. "Lockers don't do anything." I looked back at locker 307. "There's just something wrong with it. Maybe there's a squirrel trapped inside or something."

Haruki looked up at me. "Did that sound like a squirrel to you?" he asked.

"It could be a big squirrel," I said.

Haruki started walking away. "Hey!" I shouted. "What do you mean? How do you know it's not a squirrel?"

Haruki shook his head. "Just get away," he said. Then he ran down the hall toward the front doors.

Locker 307 was quiet now. I stood there for a while, not moving, hardly even breathing. Just listening. The noises had stopped.

I tiptoed back toward my own locker and picked up my backpack. Then I quietly shut my locker door, spun the dial, and backed away.

I heard something.

"Who's there?" I yelled. "Haruki, is that you?"

A soft growl came from locker 307. The growl turned into a husky voice and said, "I'll see you later."

I ran down the hall. When I reached the front door of the school, I heard a metallic sound behind me. It sounded horrible, like a locker door being ripped apart. Then I ran home fast, not daring to look back. I wanted to tell my parents about it, but then I thought about what Haruki had said. Anyone who has the locker or hears about what it does disappears. I thought about Alice Johnson and Denise Gonzales and their families.

Then I thought about how crazy it all seemed. I wondered if it could have been a trick. Haruki was really smart, after all. Maybe he'd worked up this trick, using sound effects or something.

But the next day, Haruki didn't show up at school. The day after that, our teacher stood up and made an announcement. Mrs. Langston said that Haruki Mizo and his family had moved away. He would not be at school anymore.

I didn't use my locker that day. Or the next. I told my teachers I had lost my books so they would give me new ones. I carried them around with me all day. I didn't even walk down the hall where my locker was.

Because I know what happened to Haruki and Alice and Denise, and I know it could happen to me too. That's why I'm writing this all down, Mr. Pirelli. So I can give it to you tomorrow morning as soon as school starts. So you can keep other kids safe from locker 307.

– Jeremy Hawke

The following pages were discovered in a backpack that was found on the grounds of Lovecraft Middle School by Mr. Matthew Jackson, one of the school's custodians. The backpack belonged to a former student, Jeremy Hawke. The Hawke family moved suddenly out of the area shortly after the beginning of the school year, without notifying the school. Strangely, all of the Hawke family's furniture and belongings were left in their house. None of Jeremy's friends have heard from him since.

After these papers were discovered, the custodian, Mr. Jackson, gave them to the principal, Anthony Pirelli. It has been one week, and no one has seen Mr. Jackson or Mr. Pirelli. An investigation is under way.

MICHAEL DAHL TELLS ALL

Can you imagine what a mad scientist's laboratory looks like? You've probably seen one in a movie or video game or comic book. The lab is crammed full of odds and ends, like weird electrical equipment, jars full of squishy stuff, animal skeletons, and ancient books with crumbling pages. I sometimes think of my brain as a laboratory. Mine is packed with memories, riddles, and jokes, voices of people I've met, stories from my family, pictures I've seen in books or museums. And when I start thinking of writing a story, I start picking up odd scraps, bits and pieces here and there. Like a mad scientist, I fit them together into a strange new invention. Here's a list of some of the nuts and bolts that helped build the stories in this book.

SECTION 1: DON'T LOOK BEHIND YOU!

THE FLOATING FACE

In fifth grade, I read a collection of Japanese ghost stories. The one that scared me the most told of a man walking along a bridge at night, where he sees a young woman walking ahead of him. He politely says hello, but when she turns to reply, he sees that she has no face!

WHAT THEY FOUND IN THE ALLEY

When I was in elementary school, I lived in the heart of Minneapolis with an alley running behind our house. Across the alley was a funeral home, where friends and I would go after it rained to dig up worms in the lawn. Alleys were good short cuts when biking and also made great hiding places when we played Spies. Some alleys were long and dark, filled with trash cans, rusty back doors, boarded-up windows, and pieces of old furniture. In one alley, some friends claimed they found priceless gems that had been accidentally tossed out from our local jewelry store. I searched and searched but never found any myself.

When coming up with locations for a scary story, I thought of those alleys from my childhood. Luckily nothing extraterrestrial happened to me back there — or did it?

THE GOBLIN IN THE GRASS

I confess that I use weed killer on the weeds that grow in my driveway. They push their way through the tiniest cracks to blossom with ugly blooms and jagged leaves. But this winter, while the driveway was covered with snow and ice, I've been thinking about the weed killer. All that poison. It says that it's not dangerous for pets or humans, but I'm not sure. I've begun worrying about it, like Lisa in the story. Maybe this spring, instead of spraying toxins at the weeds, I'll get down on my knees and pull them up by hand. I think I'd feel better. If there's something living under the driveway, or under my backyard garden, maybe it will feel better, too.

THE WRONG BUS

I once took the wrong bus, but I didn't end up where Lora does in the story. It was an after-school bus and I wasn't paying attention to the bus numbers. I was so used to hopping on the bus at the front of the line that I never considered the buses might sometimes be in a different order. I ended up way, way past my house and neighborhood. It was a scary experience for a kid. Especially someone like me who scares easily.

THE NOT-SO-EMPTY TENT

I've always been fascinated by Venus flytraps.
When I was five, our landlady, Mrs. Johnson,
had one sitting in the window of her upstairs
apartment. I loved visiting her and would not leave
until some poor, naïve fly landed on the hungry
pink predator. What if there were a new species
of flytrap, one that could camouflage itself from
humans? And if it grew in forests, what better way
to entice its victims than to look like something
normal, like a tent.

HELLO DARKNESS

My sister Linda is afraid of drains. My sister
Melissa is afraid of monkeys. I am afraid of dark
tunnels. What could be scarier than a tunnel that
is a drain full of monkeys? Well, there are no
monkeys in this story, but something far worse,
although it's clever like a monkey. It's something
never seen before on our planet. Never seen
because it's been hiding deep inside that drain,
practicing its voices. The title comes from a Simon
& Garfunkel song I liked when I was in seventh
grade, "The Sound of Silence."

THE BOY WHO WAS IT

Everyone has played tag or hide-and-seek at night,
right? And everyone has been It at some time.
When I was eleven, my family lived outside the

city on a double lot covered with trees and hedges and bushes, with lots of great hiding places for my friends and me. I often think about those nights and how much fun we had scaring each other. But not until a few weeks ago did I wonder what else might have been hiding in the dark, waiting to play.

WHY DAD DESTROYED THE SANDBOX

This story is actually based on a real event! My friend Aaron grew up in southern Minnesota, and when he was quite young his family moved to an old farm. There was a sandbox on the farm that Aaron and his sister played in, just like the one in the story. The sand slowly leaked out of the real one, too. When his dad investigated, Aaron and his family discovered that the sandbox had been sitting over an abandoned well. They were lucky no one fell into the hole. I decided to make my story creepier by not having a hole underneath.

SECTION 2: DON'T TURN OFF THE LIGHT!

THE DRAIN

My good friend and fellow author, Donnie Lemke, gave me the idea for this little tale. I told him that I was compiling a list of things that scare me or other people I know. My sister Linda is afraid of drains. And snakes. She's especially afraid of a snake coming out of a drain! When Donnie heard me say the word "drain," he thought of a completely different kind of drain. What if there was a storm, he asked, and the power was draining away, and . . . the story was right there!

BUMP IN THE NIGHT

When I was in fifth grade, I read and re-read Nandor Fodor's *Between Two Worlds* dozens of times, a book full of weird and paranormal events throughout recent history. One of the sections in his book is called "Of Things That Go Bump In the Night." It's an old Scottish phrase referring to any kind of creepy noise that might frighten us while we're in bed. I've never forgotten the saying. And while I was thinking about it not long ago, I thought about the different meanings of that word "bump." And then the story popped into my brain.

THE RACK

In the house where I grew up in north Minneapolis, my parents had a strange bedroom. The closets, at one end of the room, didn't have doors. They were always open. And when, as a child of four, I would sometimes slip into my parents' bed at night because I was scared by a bad dream, or by the imaginary birds outside my window, I would see those open closets. The clothes hanging there looked like people standing and watching me. I couldn't decide which was worse: going back to my own bedroom with the birds, or staying in my parents' room with the shadowy clothes-people. I did not sleep a lot in that house.

SCARING VINNY

As a kid, I was nervous about alligators because I thought they could easily squeeze under my bed due to their shape. I was also afraid of marching bears hiding in the closet. Between the reptiles and the mammals (and the scary birds outside my bedroom window) it's a wonder I was able to sleep at all! And for this story, I wanted to make two twisty endings: One, where the imaginary monsters turned out to be real. Two, where the scare-er turns into the scare-ee

SPOT ON THE CEILING

It sounds weird, but I like staring at the ceiling. After a while, the ceiling seems to disappear, the same way it happens when you lie outside and gaze up into a pure, cloudless sky. There's nothing to see except blankness. Recently I was staring up at my bedroom ceiling, and instead of drifting away, a stain caught my attention. An odd shape. "How did I not notice that spot before?" I wondered. When I said the words out loud, the word "spot" sounded like a dog's name. Then the rest of the story began unrolling itself in my imagination.

THE CREEPING WOMAN

A horror movie I saw once had a scene where a faceless woman crawled out of a TV set! I'll never forget the sight of her long black hair hanging down and her pale white arms reaching out from the flickering screen. It still gives me shivers. I must have been thinking of her when this idea popped into my head. Why Christmas? I like scary stories that contain something, a location or an event, that is normally cheerful and bright. The happy parts make the scary parts stand out and become even scarier.

THE FURNACE MAN

When I was nine, my family lived in a house with a huge old furnace in the basement, its arms reaching along the ceiling and up into the first floor vents. It had an opening large enough for a child to crawl through. We kids were always warned to stay away from it. Once my cousin Leslie stayed overnight and the unfamiliar sounds of the furnace groaning and sighing through the ducts spooked her. She had a nightmare of a man, sighing and laughing, looking at her from the vent. Those memories have stuck with me. I often wonder, was that a nightmare or something more real?

ZOMBIE CUPCAKES

As with the "The Creeping Woman" story, I like mixing up funny and scary things. Zombies are everywhere these days, in comics and on television and in films. Almost anything can become a zombie: grown-ups, kids, animals. I tried imagining something completely different from the normal walking dead guy. Something harmless and sweet. Cupcakes. Then I thought of that old saying, "You are what you eat." Which means that having dessert is now added to the list of things that frighten me.

SECTION 3: DON'T BLINK!

THE ELEVATOR GAME

This story is based on an urban legend in Japan.
I was reading about elevators, which frighten me,
and learned about this game played by young
Japanese teenagers. My version of the game is
much simpler. But in the original, the ghostly
woman, or man, stands there in the corner. I
thought it would be scarier for her to interact with
the kid who was playing the game

ERASED

I wrote a book years ago called *The Word Eater*
about a monster whose long, sticky tongue could
erase words from books or the sides of buildings.
When the word disappeared, so did the thing
the word described. For example, when the
Eater licked a name off a mailbox, the sounds
of laughter and conversation inside the house
vanished. The family disappeared. Recently, a
friend of mine wrote a story about a kid who had
a magical pencil, and everything the pencil wrote
came true. Those two stories collided in my brain
and I came up with this "reverse story" about Holli
and her eraser. Holli, by the way, is a real person.
She and her cool family live in Devon, England. If
she has a magical eraser, she hasn't said so.

I ONLY SEE CHOCOLATE

My father loved chocolate-covered cherries. My sister would always buy him a box of them for Christmas, a present he looked forward to each year. And each Christmas morning, he'd sit there eating his chocolates, while the rest of us opened our gifts. I, however, never liked cherries. Today, if I order a chocolate malt and it comes with a cherry on top — yeek! I either give it to someone else or fling it out the window and onto the grass. It's organic. It's good for the grass.

THE LOOSE NAIL

Did you know there's a village in Japan filled with life-sized dolls made of yarn? In 2005, a woman returned to her small hometown of Nagoro to find that the population was shrinking. She was lonesome, so she decided to make a yarn version of everyone who had either died or left the village. There are yarn children sitting in an abandoned school house, yarn grown-ups sitting outside their houses, and yarn farm workers standing in lonely fields. There's even a yarn wedding party. Would you want to spend a night in Nagoro? What if a gentle breeze brushed against a yarn figure and made it move? What if the figures moved when no one was looking? I don't know about you, but if I get the chance to visit Japan, I'm taking a trip to Nagoro. But I'm not staying the night.

THE MONSTER IN THE MAILBOX

Lots of writers make up stories to answer a question they have. The question that buzzed inside my head one afternoon was, "Where is the least likely place to find a monster?" I came up with various answers: a spray bottle of cheese, a car's glove compartment, a balloon, a birdhouse. Later in the day, I was checking my mailbox, and that's when I discovered the perfect hiding spot — a place people visit every day without even thinking about it.

PLEASE DON'T TOUCH THE BUS DRIVER

Scientists predict that robot-controlled cars will drive us around in the future. We'll simply step inside the car, tell the robot where we want to go, and then take a nap as we're whisked off to our location. But what if something goes wrong? That's what worries me about them. What if we end up in the wrong place, or the robot breaks down? And what if the robot doesn't look like a robot, but like a human instead? Could these robo-cars be here already and nobody has told us? Whenever I ride a bus or taxicab I stay wide-awake, because you never know . . .

ROLLER GHOSTER

My friends Christianne and Eliza suggested that I write a story about a haunted roller coaster. Roller coasters are already scary to those of us who don't like heights or moving too fast. I loved the idea, but I didn't want the ghost, or ghosts, to seem too obvious. Plus, I wanted the reader to be surprised by the ending. Hopefully that's what happened when you read this story.

MOTHER WHO

When I was quite young, I was frightened of getting lost in the grocery store. Around the same time, about age seven, I saw the original version of the movie *Invaders from Mars*. In the movie, the eleven-year-old hero learns that Martians have turned his parents into zombies. They're not his parents anymore! Nothing seemed more terrifying to my younger self. I hoped that by combining these two fears — getting lost in a store and unreal parents — the tale would be twice as creepy.

SOMETHING'S WRONG WITH LOCKER 307

This story did not come easily. It went through several re-writes. I knew I wanted to write about a letter found in a locker, a letter explaining something horrible and mysterious that had happened to a student, but I just wasn't getting it right. After two of my editors read it and gave me their feedback, the story turned into one about the actual locker itself. That's why you have editors. They help make your stories better — or in this case, spookier.

ABOUT THE AUTHOR

Michael Dahl, the author of the Library of Doom and Troll Hunters series, is an expert on fear. He is afraid of heights (but he still flies). He is afraid of small, enclosed spaces (but his house is crammed with over 3,000 books). He is afraid of ghosts (but that same house is haunted). He hopes that by writing about fear, he will eventually be able to overcome his own. So far it is not working. But he is afraid to stop. He claims that, if he had to, he would travel to Mount Doom in order to toss in a dangerous piece of jewelry. Even though he is afraid of volcanoes. And jewelry.